Pirates, Prowlers, and Cherry Pie

Pirates, Prowlers, and Cherry Pie

by

Susan Brown

Yellow Farmhouse Publications

Pirates, Prowlers, and Cherry Pie
ISBN-13: 978-1729535240
ISBN-10: 1729535240

Yellow Farmhouse Publications, Lake Stevens, WA, USA
Copyright © 2018
Publication Date: 2018

Excerpt from *Sammy and the Devil Dog* © 2017 by Susan Brown
Excerpt from *Something's Fishy at Ash Lake* © 2016 by Anne Stephenson and Susan Brown

Cover and Interior Design: Heather McIntyre
Cover&Layout, www.coverandlayout.com

Cover Photography: Girl © Cookie Studio;
Deception Pass © Heather McIntyre

For every girl and boy who has

looked for adventure!

Other books by Susan Brown you might enjoy

Sammy and the Devil Dog
Not Yet Summer
Hey, Chicken Man!
Something's Fishy at Ash Lake
An Amber & Elliot Mystery
   written with Anne Stephenson

Also try Susan Brown's fantasy books!

Dragons of Frost and Fire
Dragons of Desert and Dust
Dragons of Wind and Waves

Coming soon!

Catching Toads	*2019*
You're Dead, David Borelli	*2019*
Twelve, *a mythic fantasy*	*2019*

Pirates, Prowlers, and Cherry Pie

Contents

Chapter 1

Exiled

Fiona Smith folded her arms over her chest and scowled at the surrounding cars. As the ferry maneuvered up to the Mukilteo dock, sea gulls and crows wheeled and squawked above the crammed parking lot. In less than ten minutes, her dad would drive their car onto the ferry and it would be too late to turn around.

"Worst summer plans, ever," Fiona muttered.

"Not what any of us wanted," her dad agreed.

Frowning, Fiona twisted her fiery red hair into a tight ponytail. If she wasn't able to change her dad's mind about this looming exile, the windy gusts on the ferry would snarl her corkscrew curls into a massive knot.

"Dad, we need to go back home and think this through," Fiona urged desperately. "Explore all our options..."

Her voice faltered at her dad's look. "I don't think we've ignored any options," he said. "You may not like it much, but this plan will ensure your mom gets well."

"But without her job, we're going to be seriously broke," Fiona protested.

Her dad's hands tightened on the steering wheel. "We'll worry about money later, kiddo. Right now, we worry about your mom getting the medical treatment and rest she needs."

Fiona drummed her fingers on the door handle. Desperation made her mind click along even faster. There had to be another way – one that didn't send her into exile at her horrible Aunt Irene's house.

"I know," she said brightly. "Suppose I get a job picking blueberries? They hire twelve-year-olds. I'd be busy all day so Mom could rest up, plus there'd be all the yummy fresh fruit we can eat. It's a win-win! Can't we just go home?" She looked hopefully at her father.

Even as he smiled, Robert Smith's eyes looked exhausted. "Is this plan twenty-three or twenty-four? I've lost count."

"I just want to help," Fiona pleaded.

"I know." Her dad gave her a quick hug. "The offer's appreciated, Funny-face, but going to your aunt's for a few weeks is really the best way to help."

Fiona's shoulders sagged. "Right."

The ferry's ramp clanged down and disgorged a stream of cars and people. Most of them would drive to Seattle, thirty miles south of Mukilteo. If she'd been old enough to drive, Fiona thought, she could have stayed home and driven her mom to the weeks of appointments that lay ahead of her.

"Are you sure you have everything you need?" Her dad put the car in gear.

Fiona nodded. "Yup. I'll be fine."

"That's my girl."

As they drove onto the ferry, Fiona stared out the window, trying to mentally send her mom a picture of the white gulls soaring against the blue sky. The hospital walls might be in the way, but Fiona was determined to keep trying. Mom needed good thoughts while being treated for the cancer.

"Dad, maybe I could…"

"No, Fiona."

Her dad parked the car and together they went up the metal stairway to the open deck on the passenger level.

Clean, salty air whooshed past, whipping Fiona's hair loose from the scrunchie. She pulled curly strands from her mouth and wrinkled her nose. Her thirteen-year-old cousin, Lisa, never had messy hair…or messy anything. After a few tugs, Fiona gave up. So what if she arrived at her aunt's looking like a tornado had spit her out? Who cared if perfectly perfect Lisa rolled her eyes and made snarky comments?

"I'm going up front," Fiona said. Her father nodded.

The engine growled softly as the boat slid from its mooring. Cormorants ruffled their black feathers and watched curiously from huge wooden pylons. The shoreline shrank away. Fiona leaned on the ferry railing, loving the bite of wind on her face, remembering how this terrible trip had started.

First, there had been the scary family conference three weeks ago when her parents had explained that Mom was really sick. Mom said that she'd have to spend most of the summer either in the hospital or resting up from the treatments she was going to have.

"I'll help," Fiona said immediately. "I'll do the housework."

"I'll cook," her ten-year-old brother, Jimmy, offered. "I make awesome scrambled eggs."

Dad drummed his knuckles on the edge of the table and Mom looked like she wanted to cry. Then they dropped the rest of the bad news. They'd already talked to Mom's sisters, Rachel and Irene. As soon as school was out, Jimmy was invited to Aunt Rachel's and Fiona would go to Aunt Irene.

"All right!" Jimmy yelled.

Fiona looked from her mom to her dad. "Aunt Irene?" Her voice sounded kind of strangled.

Dad's eyes warned her. "It would be a big help to your mom," he said, "knowing that all she has to concentrate on is getting better."

"Right." Fiona shot a look at her mom. Even though she was smiling, her mother's face looked like a rubber mask – the kind with grey bags under the eyes and splotchy cheeks.

Fiona took a deep breath. "It'll be great. I'll swim every day in Aunt Irene's new pool...and, um, probably hang out with all Lisa's friends."

"Thanks, sweetie." Mom reached across the table and squeezed her daughter's hand. Fiona smiled and squeezed back.

But afterwards, Jimmy and Fiona had their own family conference in Fiona's chaotic bedroom.

"What a bummer," Jimmy said, but then he grinned. "Remember three years ago when we painted graffiti all over Lisa's bathroom with Scott's toothpaste?"

Fiona giggled. "Served her right. She gave Scott my *Beach Babe* doll to play headhunter with. The little jerk stuck its head on a stick where the tide comes in."

"It was a really stupid doll."

"True, but that's not the point."

Jimmy shrugged. "What're you going to do?"

Fiona sighed and threw herself dramatically backwards onto the bed. "Survive."

"Pay them back double for every rotten trick," Jimmy advised. "Maybe that way they'll leave you alone."

"Yeah, right." Even to Jimmy, she wouldn't admit the sick feeling in her stomach. Every time she had spent even an afternoon at her aunt's, either her cousins had bullied her or she'd accidentally ended up in six kinds of trouble. She just didn't get her cousins or her aunt. At their house, Fiona broke rules she hadn't even known existed.

If her mom hadn't been so sick, Fiona would've yelled, begged and stormed rather than go to Aunt Irene's. What was she going to do there anyway? Lisa was too cool to want her around and Scott was such a pain. Fiona didn't want to be anywhere near either of her cousins.

"Make a plan," she'd told herself firmly. "You can make this work, Fiona Smith."

Determined, she went online to find out what fun things there were to do on the island. Boutiques and beaches. She didn't have any money and Aunt Irene would never let her go off to the beach by herself. There were a couple of good pizza places – definitely a plus. But even if she had the money, she couldn't spend half the summer eating pizza.

As she clicked through an events page, Fiona ended up on the local news site.

Break-ins plague Whidbey island!

"Fantastic," Fiona muttered and with a small surge of hope, hurried downstairs to tell her dad.

"The robberies are right around where Aunt Irene lives," she pointed out. "I hope Mom won't worry about me being safe there."

"Nobody's going to rob their house. They have an alarm system." Tiredly, Dad put his book aside. "And your mom can't get better if she's worrying about you being home by yourself."

"I'm twelve, not a baby."

"That's why I know I can count on you to cooperate." He rubbed his hand over his face.

With real heroism, Fiona kept her mouth shut.

A few nights later, after reading by flashlight for way too many hours, Fiona had sneaked downstairs for a snack. When she saw the lights were still on in the kitchen, she hesitated – her parents should've been asleep by now. Fiona chewed a corkscrew of hair, then crept closer.

Her mom sounded near tears. "But Bob, what about all these bills? What are we going to do?"

"I'll put in for some overtime," Dad said. "I promise I'll work everything out. I don't want you to worry."

The tone of his voice said he didn't know how he'd work it out. Fiona sagged against the wall. It made her burn that there was no way for her to help her family – except to leave.

The kitchen chairs scraped. Fiona retreated back upstairs.

"I could've gotten a job," she muttered as she got into bed. "Twelve...nearly thirteen... isn't too young to get a job."

Too hungry to sleep, she stared at the dark ceiling, planning how she could make a lot of money. When she finally drifted off, her dreams tumbled over robbers carting away pieces of her house while she stood frozen, unable even to scream.

And despite all her ideas, she hadn't been able to make a single plan that would work.

This morning, the first day of summer vacation, they'd dropped Jimmy at Aunt Rachel's cramped apartment. Fiona had helped tote her brother's duffel and sports equipment into Ryan's room. Their eleven-year-old cousin had already cleared off the top bunk and made arrangements for Jimmy to go on a bike trek with his friends.

As Fiona and her dad got back into the car, Aunt Rachel had hugged her niece. "I wish there was room for you, honey. I'd have liked having a girl around for the summer."

Fiona wished they'd had room too. Aunt Rachel liked to have fun.

Not like Aunt Irene. She and Uncle Harold, nine-year-old Scott the brat, and thirteen-year-old Lisa the snob, lived in a huge, gorgeous house on Whidbey Island. Fiona would have rather slept on the sofa at Aunt Rachel's.

As Fiona gloomily thought about the miserable summer ahead of her, a sea gull swooped by the ferry deck, squawking for handouts. Fiona jumped and then laughed at herself. The shore was a lot closer now, looking so much like a postcard picture, Fiona couldn't imagine how a robber could fit in. Actually, she couldn't imagine how she was going to fit in either.

As the ferry nosed into the Clinton dock, Fiona and her Dad went back to the car.

"How far is it now?" Fiona asked as they drove onto the island.

"About ten minutes or so to Langley. The house is just outside town, overlooking the water."

For the next few minutes the car headed up the road to the houses on the ocean bluff, then slowed for the turn into a long driveway edged by two fieldstone pillars. A carved wooden sign, *Vickers Villa,* hung from a post.

While her Dad lifted her bags from the trunk, Fiona took a look around. At one side of the wide lawn, a man with dirty blonde hair was pulling weeds from the carefully planted flowerbeds. He stopped working for a moment to stare at Fiona. She waved. He turned his back as if he hadn't seen her.

With a shrug, Fiona looked up at the house – it was the same as she remembered from the day of the toothpaste war. Big and showy. Over to her right, Fiona spotted dapples of sunlight reflected through a row of windows.

"That must be where the new pool is," she told her dad.

He shut the trunk of the car. "Harold's done pretty well for himself. I wouldn't mind a house like this."

"Take your pick!" Fiona pointed at the long row of grand new homes crowding the bluff. "No wonder they're having so many robberies around here. Everybody's rich!"

Her dad smiled. "Will you like being one of the upper class, Funny-face?"

"I guess I'll find out."

He rang the bell and a moment later the door opened. Aunt Irene, plump and fashionably dressed, blinked her eyes nervously and smiled at them.

"Come in...come in," Aunt Irene greeted them. Fiona inhaled a cloud of expensive perfume.

"How's Nancy?" Aunt Irene asked.

Fiona's dad smiled. "She's doing okay, and she said to thank you again for helping us out with Fiona."

"We're just glad we could do something." Aunt Irene turned to her niece. "It will be lovely to have you here. And Lisa's thrilled, too...Lisa!" she called.

"I'm on the phone!" Lisa's voice echoed from another room.

"Fiona's here!"

There was no answer.

"Oh, dear...well, everything's ready for you...." She glanced anxiously at her niece. "I'm afraid Scott is spending the afternoon at a friend's, but I insisted Lisa stay home and wait until you arrived, Fiona. And I've told her that she's to take you along with her everywhere...."

Fiona felt her face heat up. Guaranteed now that Lisa would make the summer horrible.

"Let's have a cool drink on the patio. I'll get Marcus to carry your bags upstairs."

"I can do it," Fiona said. "Who's Marcus?"

"Our housekeeper's son. He's a nice boy." She spotted her daughter walking slowly toward them, her phone still in hand, her eyes firmly on the screen. "Oh, good. Lisa, can you show Fiona where to take her things? Robert, we'll get that cool drink. Harold is around here somewhere...."

Still talking, Aunt Irene led Fiona's dad toward the back of the house.

The girls stared awkwardly at each other for a moment, and then Lisa shoved her phone in her pocket and picked up one of Fiona's bags. "You're sleeping upstairs with me." She started toward the curving oak stairway, and then turned around. "I'm really sorry about your mom."

"Yeah, thanks."

"But don't think I'm going to spend my summer baby-sitting you."

"I'm twelve," Fiona snapped. "I don't need baby-sitting."

"Good." For the first time her cousin smiled. "This way." She led Fiona upstairs and into the first door at the top.

The bedroom was huge, with blue carpet and white and blue wallpaper. The twin beds had carved oak headboards and frilly white bedspreads. Fiona dropped her bags, made a bee-line to the dormer window between the beds, and kneeled on the window seat. "This is incredible."

The Cascade Mountains rose mistily blue in the distance. The green lawn ended in a bluff that dropped down to a wide beach where the ocean lapped and surged over the golden sand.

Lisa leaned on the windowsill beside Fiona. "That's the Saratoga Passage. Pirates used to sail around here and hide in the San Juan Islands."

"Real pirates?" Fiona wasn't sure whether her cousin was setting her up.

"Yes. Sometimes people even find gold coins washed up on the beaches."

"Like from buried treasure?" Fiona tried to keep her voice neutral. Buried treasure would be amazing.

Lisa nodded. "In fact, about ten years ago a couple of university researchers used the library's old maps to track down a pirate base. They told Dad they found a broken up pirate chest."

"That is so cool." Fiona rested her chin in her hands and gazed out the window. "I can just see it – ghost ships sailing under the moon. Year after year…searching for their lost treasure…."

"Get a grip," Lisa retorted. "And don't forget this room is mine. Keep your things on your side and we'll get along."

She turned on her heel and left.

"I can't wait." Fiona looked back out over the water and tried to send a mind picture of the mountains and blue waves to her mother.

Somehow, she didn't think she got through.

Chapter 2

House of Horrors

"Fiona," Lisa complained. "This is boring! It's stupid to swim back and forth and back and forth."

Fiona stood up in the chest-high water of the pool and pulled back her goggles. Blue and green sun diamonds sparkled on the surface. "We've only been in the pool twenty minutes."

"Twenty-five and I'm leaving. I have a life, you know." Her cousin grabbed a towel and walked out.

Fiona readjusted her goggles and dove under. Who cared about her cousin's life? Fiona clenched her teeth and stroked harder and harder, making herself go faster and faster. In September, when she was finally home, when Mom was better and everything was back to normal, she'd try out for the school swim team.

"*Fiona! Fiona Smith!*" Four laps later, Aunt Irene's voice pierced the *bubble-stroke-breath* rhythm.

Fiona blew the air out in a rush of bubbles, and then surfaced. Her aunt's body looked wavy through the goggles.

"Fiona, come out of the pool at once!"

Fiona pulled off her goggles to argue and then firmly shut her mouth.

"Be good," Dad had said as he left. His eyes said a lot more.

Fiona swam slowly to the side of the pool.

"What are you doing?" Aunt Irene demanded.

This has to be a trick question. "Swimming?" Fiona ventured.

"Alone!" Aunt Irene's hands were on her hips.

Fiona looked around the pool deck. "Yup. Not a mermaid in sight."

Aunt Irene stared at her niece as if she were very, very weird.

"That was a joke," Fiona explained. She could feel her face getting hot.

"But dear, that's so dangerous," Aunt Irene said. "The house rule is that you may not swim alone."

"Nobody told me!"

"Oh..." Aunt Irene took a deep breath. "I know it will be difficult at first to adjust to a different household, Fiona, but I'm responsible...and your mother...you will try to obey our rules, won't you, dear?"

Reluctantly, Fiona nodded.

"Wonderful!" Aunt Irene beamed, turned to leave, but then hesitated. "If you need anything Fiona, please feel free to ask. Your Uncle Harold and I hope this summer will be pleasant for all of us." She smiled again and left.

Fiona pulled herself out of the pool and sat on the edge, kicking the water. What if Lisa refused to swim with her? Would Scott be considered a "someone" for the swimming rule? She'd better find out.

Without bothering to dry off, Fiona ran bare-footed across the tiled deck, into the sunroom, and then detoured through the pantry toward the kitchen, looking for her aunt.

The sandy-haired man she'd seen earlier was taking a piece of paper off the kitchen bulletin board.

"Excuse me!" Fiona said. "Do you know where my Aunt Irene is?"

The man whirled around, dropping the push pin. His face flushed red. He shoved the paper into his pocket.

"Uh...no. I haven't seen her," he said. "I was...um...getting a drink of water." He opened a cupboard, took out a glass, and went over to the sink.

"*You!* What've you done to my floors!"

Fiona and the man both jumped. A short, dumpy woman wearing a black uniform bustled into the kitchen.

"Just getting a drink, Mrs. Glee." He hastily put the glass down and practically dashed out the kitchen door.

Mrs. Glee glared first at Fiona and then at the trail of puddled water behind her.

Fiona twisted to look. "I, uh, guess I should have dried off."

"As if I don't have enough to do around here...." The woman reached into a cupboard for a mop. "I suppose you're that cousin of Lisa's."

"I'm Fiona Smith. Pleased to meet you, um...Mrs. Glee." Fiona faltered. Bravely, she held out her hand.

The woman sniffed and instead of shaking hands, shoved the mop into Fiona's palm. "I'm the housekeeper, not the nursemaid. I work for Mr. and Mrs. Vickers – not you kids, understand?"

"Yes."

"Good. You make a mess, you clean it up. Got that?"

"I got it," Fiona sighed.

The housekeeper poured herself a cup of coffee and then left the kitchen.

"Mrs. Glee...hah!" Fiona muttered. She swiped at the tile floor with the mop, and then followed her trail backwards.

She'd bet anything her brother Jimmy wasn't mopping a floor at Aunt Rachel's.

With a last swish over the tiles, Fiona put the mop back in the cupboard and ran upstairs to get changed – before she made another mistake.

Her cousin was sitting on the window seat, sketching. Fiona quickly peeled out of her wet swimsuit, pulled on shorts and a t-shirt, then stretched out on her stomach on the bed. She folded the pillow and propped up her elbows and chin on it.

"Who's the guy with the sandy hair?"

Lisa's pencil moved rapidly across the paper. "Bruce Lansford. Dad hired him a couple of weeks ago to do the gardening."

"He's a little strange."

Lisa nodded and turned to Fiona. "He's been hanging around the area for the last month or so – looking for odd jobs. He gives me the creeps."

Fiona sat up. "Do you think he's a criminal or something? Maybe he's connected to the break-ins."

"The cops don't seem to think so." Lisa scowled. "They've already decided who's guilty and Bruce is picking up all his jobs. See." She turned her sketchpad to show Fiona. A pirate hung from the riggings of a sailing ship – a pirate with Bruce's face.

Fiona laughed. "That's great."

Lisa smiled and flipped to a clean page. "A modern San Juan pirate."

"And Mrs. Glee is a vigilante. I just got nailed for water crimes – I dripped across the floor."

Lisa grimaced and lowered her sketchpad. "Once she made me clean the entire fridge after I spilled some pop. I mean, I cleaned up the pop but Mrs. Glee said I had to do the whole fridge, just to be sure."

"Gross! How can you stand her?"

Lisa shrugged. "What choice do I have? She works for my mother..."

"...not for us kids!" Fiona finished. "Does she live around here?"

"In the cottage above the boathouse with her son, Marcus."

"How old is Marcus? What's he like?" Fiona asked. Maybe there was someone besides Lisa to hang out with.

Lisa shrugged. "He's sixteen and okay, I guess. The other kids like him, but he lets on that his mom rents the cottage for the waterfront view. Not like anyone cares."

She started drawing again. Fiona lay back and stared at the ceiling. Her stomach growled.

"When's dinner?"

"When Mrs. Glee rings the dinner bell."

Fiona sighed. Might as well write to her mom. She poked around in her bag for her tablet and began typing an email. Finally, the dinner bell sounded. It was all Fiona could do not to tear down the stairs. Lisa didn't seem to be in any rush.

One look around the table and Fiona could see why. The bowls and platters held limp green beans, salad with watery blue cheese dressing, burned lamb chops, and sticky rice. Fiona took a lot of rice.

Scott had come back from his friend's. He sat opposite Fiona beside his sister. Every time Fiona glanced his way, he let his mouth hang open while he chewed.

House of horrors, Fiona decided.

"These chops are tough as plywood," Uncle Harold grumbled.

"Hush," Aunt Irene whispered.

Mrs. Glee stomped in, dropped a basket of rolls on the table, and then stomped out again.

"Did you hear about the break-in at the Wadsworth's?" Aunt Irene asked.

"Hmm?"

"There've been *more* robberies?" Fiona laid down her fork.

"Oh, yes. All poor Mary's jewelry was stolen last night. They'd gone to the ballet in Seattle."

Fiona frowned. "What about clues? Do the police have any leads?"

"Everybody *knows* it was the boy who does odd jobs, but the police let him go – again! The Mazursky's were robbed a week ago and that boy does chores for them too."

"Did the police question him?" Fiona took another helping of rice and tried to hide her beans with it.

Lisa glared at them both. "Derek does chores for most of the houses along the beach. He isn't a thief!"

"You don't know about such things, dear," Aunt Irene said. "Please eat your dinner."

"Is Mrs. Glee having a bad night?" Fiona ventured.

"I beg your pardon?"

"The food seems a little...overcooked."

Uncle Harold snorted with laughter. "It is every night, unless it's half raw."

"Oh, Harold! It's not that bad..." Aunt Irene cast an anxious glance at the swinging door leading to the kitchen.

Lisa watched her cousin from under lowered lashes. Scott stuck out a rice-coated tongue. Fiona grimaced back at him. To her surprise, Uncle Harold winked and passed her the bread basket.

"Have a roll, Fiona. I bought them fresh at the bakery today."

Fiona gratefully took two. Scott snagged a couple as well. Lisa however, slowly twirled limp beans around on her plate, not noticing.

"Mom," Lisa said finally, "The Friday Night Club is starting tonight at Ginger Bocci's house."

Aunt Irene frowned. "Lisa, dear, with the robberies...and that club is such a mixed group."

"The club's completely chaperoned," Lisa pleaded. "All my friends are going. Even Tiffany's mom lets her go. You know how strict Mrs. Mirosa is."

Aunt Irene hesitated.

"Marcus says," Scott offered thickly, his mouth stuffed with bread. "That that's where the cool dudes pick up the babes." He grinned at his mother's horrified expression.

"Scott...your language! Babes? Oh, dear! I don't like the sound of that."

"Mom, it's not like that!" Lisa wailed. "We just listen to music and talk and Mr. Bocci's going to build a bonfire on the beach. And

Ginger's parents are going to be right there the whole time!"

"Let the girl have some fun, Irene," Uncle Harold intervened. "Besides, it'll be good for Fiona to meet some of the young people around here. Even the...um, cool dudes."

Lisa's eyes swung toward her cousin. "But Fiona wasn't invited. Nobody knows her and... and..." The cousins glared at each other. Fiona took another roll and slowly ripped it apart.

"Is there a problem, Lisa?" Her father's eyebrows rose.

Lisa scowled, but gave in. "No, Dad."

Fiona knifed some butter onto the roll. "I'd rather stay home and read, thanks."

"Nonsense," Uncle Harold said. "You'll be here all summer, so you should make some friends. Isn't that right, Irene?"

"Of course, dear."

Uncle Harold got up from the table. "Good. Then it's settled."

Scott smirked at his sister. "I wanna go too."

"In your dreams, you little creep." Lisa thrust away from the table and left the room.

"Oh dear," Aunt Irene sighed. "Fiona you'd better hurry and get ready. Lisa's like her father. She hates to be kept waiting."

Just in time, Fiona remembered her dad's warning about getting along. "I'll hurry," she answered. "Should I take my dishes to the kitchen?"

Aunt Irene smiled. "Thank you, dear. But Mrs. Glee looks after that."

Fiona left. In the bedroom, Lisa was taking a designer shirt out of her closet. "Do you want some help fixing your hair?" she asked. "You look like you stuck your finger in an electric socket."

"I can do my own hair."

"Good. I don't want you to embarrass me."

"You mean perfection can be embarrassed?" Fiona grabbed a scrunchie, pulled her hair into a tight ponytail and went into the bathroom. She twisted the taps, sending a spray of steamy water into the tub.

"I'm cooperating," she sighed as she stripped down for her shower. "But I don't like it!"

Susan Brown

Chapter 3

The Friday Night Club

With profound envy, Fiona watched as, with a flick of her fingers, Lisa flipped her hair perfectly in place.

Fiona wrinkled her nose at her own reflection. Her hair didn't have the finger-in-the-electric-socket look now. It was more a red-algae-seaweed-washed-up-on-the-beach look.

She sighed and rooted through her bag for a pair of clean jeans and her favorite *Save the Whales* t-shirt. Maybe the creases would shake out after she'd worn it awhile. To finish her outfit, she took out her most prized possessions – a Native American leather belt with a beaded buckle and matching hair clips.

Determinedly Fiona brushed her hair and set the clips in place. Their blue and white pattern shone in her red curls. Not so bad after all.

When she turned around, Lisa was watching her.

"Nice beadwork," Lisa said.

"Thanks. You look great."

Lisa smiled quickly. "I do?"

"You always do," Fiona retorted.

Lisa's smile widened. "Thanks."

The two girls hurried down the staircase. Feeling like she was being watched, Fiona whipped around just in time to see Scott disappear behind a door. She grinned. In some ways the little rat was just like her brother Jimmy.

Maybe the summer could be bearable after all. There might even be some nice kids at the party tonight. For good luck, Fiona patted one of the barrettes holding back her hair.

The girls hurried out the front door. It was still light, but the sun was close to the horizon. On the far side of the property, by the swimming pool, Fiona caught sight of Bruce trimming the hedges with power shears. The results were pretty ragged.

"He works late," Fiona said.

Lisa shrugged. "Most of the time he doesn't even show up until afternoon, then he works until it's too dark to see." She speeded up. "Move it, Fiona. I don't want to miss the bonfire."

The girls hurried down the driveway and turned onto the road.

"Who comes to this Club?" Fiona asked.

"Everybody. Not just the kids on the bluff," Lisa said. "The Friday Night Club is the best part of the summer. Last August, I met...." She hesitated.

"Who?"

"Oh, a bunch of kids. Some really nice ones."

They followed the road for close to a mile. A couple of cars loaded with young people went by and hooted their horns. Lisa laughed and waved. The two cousins finally turned into a long driveway leading to a huge house, ablaze with lights.

"This is it," Lisa said. "Ginger Bocci and I are enemies, but her folks have a lot of money so Mom says I should cultivate her." Lisa tossed her head. "I don't cultivate anybody unless I like them." She stared challengingly at Fiona.

Fiona looked at her blankly. "I thought you cultivated a garden, not people."

Lisa laughed. Even before they got to the door, they could hear the music blasting. A flustered-looking maid answered the door.

"They're starting in the family room, thataway," she said.

Lisa went in the direction the woman indicated.

"Thanks!" Fiona smiled.

The maid smiled back. "You're welcome, honey."

Fiona had to practically run to keep up with Lisa. They went down a hall tiled with black and white marble, then into a long room overlooking the Saratoga Passage. It was half full of kids from Fiona and Lisa's age, all the way to about eighteen. An athletic-looking man in jeans and a sweatshirt was handing out icy cans of pop from a big cooler. Baskets of chips and popcorn were going hand-to-hand around the room.

"Hello, Mr. Bocci," Lisa called.

"Hi, Lisa," he replied. "Glad you could make it."

Lisa immediately headed over to a group of kids, leaving Fiona at the door.

"Hi there," Mr. Bocci said to her. "I don't think we've met. I'm Carl Bocci."

He held out his hand. Embarrassed, Fiona shook it. "I'm Fiona Smith, Lisa's cousin. I'm staying here for the summer."

"Everybody, listen up!" Mr. Bocci called out. Fiona wanted to sink into a hole. "This is Fiona. Ginger, make sure she meets everyone."

A girl with blonde hair and freckles came over. "Want something to drink?" She asked. "Or do you want to meet everyone first?"

Fiona shrugged.

Ginger smiled. "Come on, then."

She took her around, saying everybody's names which Fiona mostly forgot right away. She remembered Lisa mentioning Tiffany, and a girl named Cathy smiled at her. Everybody else said, "Hi!" then went back to talking with their friends. Most of the conversations were about the break-ins.

"My mom had her pearl necklace stolen," Ginger said dramatically. "And the emerald bracelet she inherited."

"It's so scary." Tiffany shivered. "We were asleep while someone was going through our stuff, and we didn't even know. I'm afraid to go to bed at night."

"You ought to get a dog," one of the boys said. "A dog would bark."

"The Mazurskys have a dog," Cathy pointed out. "And they got robbed anyway."

"Because the dog knew the robber." Ginger's eyes narrowed. "Hey, Fiona, have you met Derek yet?"

Fiona shook her head. "No. Will he be here tonight?"

"Derek...in this house? Not a chance. Everybody knows he's the thief."

Fiona frowned. "But Lisa said he's innocent."

"She's got it for him so bad," Ginger said. Her smile was cold. "No matter what the evidence proves against Derek, Lisa ignores it."

"But the police don't have proof against him," Cathy protested.

Ginger arched her eyebrows. "Excuse me, but isn't he the one who's in practically everybody's house because he does odd jobs for them? Isn't that a little too convenient?"

"I don't know..." Tiffany said.

"I do!" Ginger took a drink of her pop. "I *know* Derek's the thief!"

Fiona saw her cousin's head turn toward them, then she strode over.

"What are you talking about?" Lisa demanded.

Ginger grinned. "We were just telling Fiona about Derek...and how much you like him."

Lisa's face reddened, but her eyes were icy. "I like a lot of people."

"That can be dangerous these days."

"What do you mean, Ginger?"

The girl's green eyes gleamed. "You haven't been robbed yet," she said. "If I were you, I'd be watching for somebody who might be sizing up my house."

"Like who?"

Ginger smiled. "Everybody knows Derek's been hanging around you...and everybody knows Derek's the thief."

"That's a lie." Lisa's eyes flashed. "But you keep saying he did it. And you'd better stop!"

Ginger put her hands on her hips. "It's a free country. I can say whatever I want!"

Astonished, Fiona looked from one girl to the other. For a minute, it looked like Lisa was going to say a lot more, but just then Mr. Bocci called out, "Time to collect driftwood, gang. We're aiming for a really huge bonfire!"

Laughing and yelling, the kids streamed out the sliding glass doors, onto the lawn, then down wooden steps to the beach. Ginger tossed her head and stalked away. Fiona would've followed, but Lisa caught her arm.

"I told you Ginger's my enemy! Why were you talking to her?"

Fiona yanked her arm back. "Because it's a free country, remember, and I can talk to whoever I want! Besides, she didn't dump me at the door!"

The cousins glared at each other.

"Come on, kids!" Mr. Bocci urged them. "You'll miss all the fun!"

Fun, decided Fiona a while later, did not describe the Friday Night Club.

Everyone collected driftwood until it was too dark to see, and then gathered around the pyre of wood. Fiona hung around Ginger, but except for handing her another can of pop, the other girl ignored her. Fiona wandered away and sat on a log at the edge of the firelight. Slowly she sipped her drink.

Are we having fun yet? she thought. Her own friends were probably having a sleepover tonight, watching a movie and pigging out on popcorn.

She wondered how her mom was doing.

Mr. Bocci lit the stacked wood. Everybody cheered as the fire spat and crackled, then flamed into the night.

On the far side of the fire, Lisa sat with a group of girls. They glanced in Fiona's direction and burst out laughing. Fiona squirmed uncomfortably. A moment later Lisa and Tiffany, each holding a flashlight, left the others and ran over.

"You've got to come with us!" Tiffany declared. She laughed excitedly.

"Why?" Fiona looked from one to the other.

"Come on!" Lisa pulled her cousin to her feet. "Hurry up!"

Tiffany and Lisa each took an arm and pulled Fiona along the dark beach, away from the bonfire. The beams from the flashlights bobbed wildly across the sand. For the first time tonight Fiona began to feel that something fun would happen.

"What is it?" she demanded.

"Shh! It's a secret!" Lisa declared.

"You'll love it," Tiffany giggled. "Trust us."

They were going so fast now, Fiona had to practically run to keep up. But the girls were giggling and laughing so hard, Fiona decided it couldn't be an emergency – or that much of a secret.

After about ten minutes, Lisa and Tiffany staggered to a walk and still giggling, stopped.

"We're going to show you the most incredible secret," Tiffany whispered. "Shut your eyes."

"Why?" Fiona demanded. She twisted around to look back. The bluff hid the bonfire. Except for the flashlights, the beach was pitch dark.

"It's kind of a pirate thing," Lisa told her.

Tiffany giggled. "We found out how they guarded their treasure. But you have to shut your eyes."

Fiona hesitated, then reluctantly obeyed. She didn't want to be a spoilsport. "Now what?"

"Count to a hundred while we get it ready."

...One...two...three...

Lisa and Tiffany kept giggling, but they seemed to be moving away.

...Seven...eight...

Maybe they'd found some hidden pirate treasure. Were they digging by the bluff?

...Twelve...thirteen...

What was it, Fiona had read about pirates?

...Eighteen...nineteen...

Pirates always left a guard.

...Twenty...twenty-one...

One of their own men! They abandoned one of their men! Fiona's eyes flew open.

The beach was utterly dark – no moon, no stars, no flashlights. Tiffany and Lisa had gone. The only sound was the soft *lap, lap* of the flowing tide. The blackness was so thick Fiona couldn't make out either the looming wall of the bluff or the cold edge of the water.

A shiver ran from her neck to her toes. She was lost!

Chapter 4

Who Said Life's Fair?

The shoreline was pitch black. Fiona held her breath, listening. Only the sigh of wind. The wet murmur of creeping waves. The gaspy sound of her own breathing.

"Don't scream," she told herself. "Just figure out how to get back...and then pay Lisa back double."

Hands held out in front of her, Fiona took a few steps. Did the water sound closer? A few more steps. An icy cold wavelet washed over her shoes. Fiona yelped and jumped back.

Panting, she stood still. If the water was in front of her, then the bonfire was to the left. Taking a deep breath, she walked slowly through the darkness along the hard-packed sand.

"It's only the night...the moon will be out any minute..." she chanted. "*Aagh!*" Too close to the water again. Her shoes would never be the same.

Then her foot caught on a half-buried chunk of driftwood. She pitched forward and sprawled in the sand.

A wave sluiced over her. Her toe throbbed.

Fiona got up and kept walking. Great. Now she was sopping wet as well as lost.

"Lisa, you'll pay," she ground out.

Finally the beach curved and the bonfire winked into sight. Lisa, Tiffany and two of their friends sat on the driftwood log. Fiona stalked over.

"See any pirates?" Tiffany giggled.

"Are you okay?" Cathy asked. "Lisa, how could you be so mean to your own cousin? I would've died."

"I'm fine." Fiona faked a smile. "Great joke, Lisa."

"I thought so." Her cousin smiled too, but Fiona didn't think she looked very happy. That suited Fiona fine.

"See you!" She walked away. *You barracuda!*

Fiona stomped up to the road and walked the length of about three houses before noticing that the road was also pitch black. She groaned. No streetlights on country roads and the hedges and trees blocked the house lights.

Footsteps! Someone else was out here!

A twig cracked.

Something rustled in the bushes.

The burglar! Fiona held her breath.

A flashlight snapped on. "Fiona!"

"*Scott?*"

Her cousin stepped out from the bushes and held the flashlight under his chin, making his face look ghoulish.

"The spook look is definitely you." Fiona laughed – only a little hysterically. "What are you doing here?"

"Looking for you." Scott shone the light around the road.

"Why?"

"Lisa told me she was going to dump you."

A red glare of anger heated up her face. Fiona took a deep breath.

"Can I hold the flashlight?" Scott handed it over. Fiona gripped the handle tightly – she might never let go again.

Scott picked up a stick and whipped it into a ditch. A burst of flying insects darted through the beam. "Lisa doesn't want you butting into her secrets."

"What secrets?"

He made a zipping motion across his mouth.

"You're a little ratface."

Scott grinned. Fiona couldn't help but smile back.

When they got back to the house – Fiona limping slightly and Scott dashing up and down the road – most of the lights were off. At Scott's sign, Fiona handed over the flashlight. They could see the silhouette of Uncle Harold making notes on some kind of bound report. Scott motioned Fiona toward the wing that housed the pool.

Trying not to giggle, they sneaked around the side. A light from Mrs. Glee's cottage shone over the grass. Scott switched off his flashlight and slid open the glass door. Once inside, he locked it behind them.

Moving silently, Fiona followed her cousin. In the pantry, he suddenly slammed backward into her, finger frantically held to his lips. Mrs. Glee, untying her apron, went past them toward the living room. She didn't notice as the two kids dove under the pantry table.

"There's a cup of coffee left, Mr. Vickers," they heard her say. "You want it, or should I pour it out?"

The papers rustled. "I'll get it in a minute, Mrs. Glee."

"All right. 'Night then." Mrs. Glee came back, hung up her apron, and went out the kitchen door.

"Whew!" Scott whispered.

Stifling their laughter, they ran through the kitchen, tore into the hall and raced up the stairs. They heard the key turn in the front door as they hit the upstairs hall.

"I'm home," Lisa called.

"Did you girls have a good time?" Uncle Harold answered from the living room. His paper rustled again.

"It was okay. I'm going to get something to eat."

Scott gave a thumbs up, then disappeared into his room. In her own room, Fiona whipped off her wet clothes, tossed them under the bed, and pulled on her nightgown. By the time Lisa came upstairs, Fiona was pretending to be asleep.

She kept her eyes shut and her breathing slow while her cousin got ready for bed. A few moments later Uncle Harold's footsteps sounded in the hall. The lights clicked off.

For a while, Fiona lay staring at the dark ceiling, thinking about home. Tomorrow she'd buy a postcard in town, one with killer whales – orcas – slicing black and white through the waves. Mom would like that a lot.

When Fiona woke the next morning, Lisa was already up and gone.

Groggily, she checked the clock: 8:06. What had Dad said? Oh yeah...considerate guests don't lie around in bed all day.

"Rise and shine, Fiona," she muttered.

She staggered to the shower in the adjoining bathroom, then considerably more awake, chose a fresh *Save the Rain Forests* t-shirt. For a moment Fiona wondered what to do with the soggy clothes lying under the bed. She hadn't seen a hamper.

"Oh, to heck with it."

Conscientiously, she drew up the blankets and bedspread. The overhang hid the clothes. They'd keep until she had a chance to check on the laundry rules.

Downstairs, breakfast had been served on the white wrought-iron table on the patio. Uncle Harold was buried in a newspaper. Aunt Irene slowly sipped coffee.

Fiona gazed past the lawn to the blue, blue sky and satin rise and fall of the waves. She took a deep, clean breath.

"Good morning!" She slid into a chair.

"Hmm..." Uncle Harold grunted.

Aunt Irene blinked as though the words were painful. "Good morning, dear," she managed.

Fiona smiled and poured herself a glass of orange juice. Then she heaped her plate with bacon and toast.

"Lisa's sketching on the beach," Aunt Irene offered. "She takes her breakfast down there every morning."

To prevent herself from blurting out what she thought of her cousin, Fiona bit hard into her toast. She swiveled around to watch some crows squawking in the low trees at the end of the lawn.

What was Lisa doing on the beach? Fiona picked up a piece of bacon with her fingers and nibbled the end. One of Lisa's stupid secrets, perhaps? Fiona took another bite.

If she could find out what those secrets were, it might keep Lisa off her back for the rest of the summer. She'd promised Dad, that one way or another, she'd get along with her cousin. A little blackmail might be what she needed to keep that promise. Hurriedly, Fiona ate the rest of her breakfast.

"May I be excused, please?"

"Certainly, dear," Aunt Irene murmured.

Fiona smiled in the direction of Uncle Harold's paper and bounded toward the edge of the patio.

"Fiona...not over the railing!" Aunt Irene called – too late.

"Sorry," Fiona called back.

She found Lisa about a quarter of a mile down the beach, sitting on a driftwood log with a sketchpad in her lap. A boy, about fifteen, with shaggy hair and shabby clothes sat beside her. A dog with black fur and white freckled paws rested his head on the boy's knee. Lisa's friend slowly stroked the dog's head with one hand as he gestured toward the bay with the other.

"...look at the dark shape against the light on the water," he was saying.

Fiona followed their gaze. A great blue heron stood motionless in the shallows. Suddenly it took several running steps, spread its vast wings and wheeled into the air.

"Oh..." Fiona sighed.

"You scared it!" Lisa accused.

"No, she didn't," the boy said. The dog jumped up and barked. "Quiet, Pixie! See, there's a boat just coming round the point." He smiled at Fiona. "Are you going to introduce us, Lisa?"

"This is my cousin, Fiona. She's spending the summer with us." Lisa turned away, and frowning, kept sketching.

"Hi, Fiona. I'm Derek Lopez." He stood up and held out his hand.

"You're Derek?" Fiona hesitated a fraction of a second, but then shook hands. His was warm and strong. Was a robber's hand like that?

"Are you an artist, like Lisa?" he asked.

Fiona shook her head and resisted the urge to rub her hand on her jeans. "I never got past stick men. Is that your dog?"

"No. Pixie's a stray, but Lisa and I've been feeding her."

Derek tossed a stick for the dog. He and Lisa both smiled when Pixie trotted back with it.

"I gotta go," he said. "I'm due at the Mazursky's...that is, if they haven't fired me by now."

"It isn't fair!" Lisa said in a low voice.

"Who said life's fair?" Derek shrugged. "Nice to meet you, Fiona."

He jogged along the wet sand, then cut through a steep tangle of salmonberry bushes up to the road. Pixie dropped the stick and followed.

"Can I see?" Fiona craned her neck towards Lisa's sketchpad. Her cousin flipped it shut, stood up, and feet angrily kicking through the sand, headed back toward the house. Fiona took a deep breath, counted to ten, and then followed.

"I'm going into town to get a postcard for Mom," Fiona said when she caught up. "Want to go?"

"No."

Fiona shrugged. "Suit yourself."

Uncle Harold had left the house, but Aunt Irene was talking on her phone. Scott happily gulped mouthfuls of cereal while reading a comic book.

"I can't believe it," Aunt Irene was saying. "He disconnected their security system?"

Fiona loitered by the table hoping her Aunt would notice her.

"...and just when are the police going to do something? Isn't that why we pay taxes?" Her eyes suddenly focused on Fiona. "Could you hold on just a minute, Caroline?...Oh, I know...yes...Now you won't forget our little party on Thursday, will you?...All right, I'll call you back later.... 'Bye!"

She thumbed the off button. "What is it, dear?"

"Would it be okay if I go into town to buy a postcard?" Fiona asked.

"Can I go?" Scott demanded. Bits of cereal puffed across the table.

"Well..." her aunt hesitated.

"I don't mind Scott coming," Fiona said. Her cousin grinned at her. "We'll stick together."

Aunt Irene gave her permission. Scott swallowed the rest of his cereal and tore upstairs to get his money. Fiona went to her own room, stopped to stare at her reflection, and sighed. If only she could make her hair look as good as Lisa's did.

"Comin'?" Scott called from the door.

Fiona picked up her bag and went with him.

The walk to the main part of town took about twenty minutes. The ocean view was blocked most of the way by stone fences and high hedges. On the other side, thickets of thorny salmonberry and blackberry mounded over scrub meadows. Thin trees poked up through the tangle.

"I caught a snake over here once," Scott confided.

Fiona made a face. "Great! Too bad Jimmy isn't here – he'd love it!"

Scott scowled. "I wouldn't show Jimmy – he thinks he's so great because he's a year older'n me."

Fiona stopped. "That's not true. You're always rotten to him."

Scott shrugged and kept going. "He started it."

Fiona hurried to catch up. "Well, next time you see him, you don't be rotten and I'll tell him not to give you a hard time. Deal?"

Scott picked up a stone and whipped it into the brambles. "Deal," he agreed.

At the pharmacy and gift shop, Scott headed directly to a rack of toys. By the time Fiona chose some postcards, Scott had lined up at the counter. Clutched in his hands was a fluorescent green and yellow water rifle loaded with double water tanks.

"That's incredible!" Fiona exclaimed.

He flashed a grin and handed a wad of crumpled bills to the cashier.

"All the kids are buying these," the woman said. "We sell out faster than we can stock them."

"I've been trying to get a 580 for three weeks," Scott said. "Good thing we came into town."

"Right." Fiona paid for the postcards and bought them both ice cream bars. All the way home, Scott practiced commando style raids on lurking rabbits and skulking crows.

"What are you going to do with it?" Fiona asked.

Scott grinned and aimed at a dragonfly zipping past. "Pow!...Once I fill the tanks, I'm going to keep it handy in case anybody breaks into our house."

Fiona felt a little shiver of fear. "No one's going to break in. The house has an alarm system."

Scott practiced the pumping action on the barrel. "All the new houses do. But Marcus says they're no good. That's why the thief can break in so easy."

As they turned into the driveway, Fiona resisted the urge to peer around for any suspicious looking types – maybe in black ski masks.

"Well, a water gun won't stop anybody. Want to go swimming?"

"Nope. I'm going to fill up and go to Michael's." He headed over to the side of the house where a hose was coiled. Fiona went inside.

Up in her room, she found Lisa sketching on the window seat.

"Want to go swimming?" she tried again.

Lisa pulled her gaze from the window. "Leave me alone! I don't want to do anything. Can't you figure that out?"

"Why don't you drop dead!" Fiona stalked out of the room. Down on the beach, she kicked sand and seaweed in every direction.

How could Mom and Dad have sent her here?

Abruptly Fiona stopped kicking. What if the only picture she got through to her Mom was an angry one?

Fiona made herself think of killer whales flashing through the water...and pirate ships with white sails stretching against blue sky.

With a deep breath, Fiona sat down on a driftwood log. She wouldn't let Lisa get to her. She wouldn't.

Chapter 5

Cherry Pie and Prowlers

Fiona rolled over and sat up, wide-awake. She could hear Lisa breathing peacefully across the room. And she could hear her own stomach growling.

Dinner had been spaghetti. The overcooked noodles had stuck together and the sauce had lots of onions in it. Fiona hated onions.

Her stomach growled again.

Behaving herself didn't include starving, Fiona decided. Quietly she slipped out of bed and padded barefoot across the room. The hallway was dark. Using the wall to guide her fingertips, she felt for the oak banister, then slowly crept downstairs.

Pitch black. All the drapes were drawn, but Fiona felt a cold draft over her bare feet and she could smell the tang of salt water. Someone must've left a window open.

"Oof!" Fiona smacked her leg on a table pushed against the wall.

A second later, she heard a muffled sound. Holding her breath, she rubbed her shin and listened.

Nothing. She firmly pushed down a shiver of fear. A breeze must've rustled Uncle Harold's stack of legal papers. What else could it be?

Through the door ahead, she could see the faint gleam of moonlight on shiny appliances. Nervously, Fiona wiped her palms on her pajamas. Her target lay straight ahead.

"Don't stop now, Fiona," she whispered. Darting into the kitchen, she made a beeline for the fridge. A quick tug on the double doors, and....

Heaven at last, Fiona thought.

The refrigerator light illuminated cans of pop, leftover deli chicken, cold cuts, and a large cherry pie with a third already gone. Nobody would notice if another piece was missing, would they? And why hadn't any of this good stuff been offered at dinner?

This was the weirdest house Fiona had ever seen.

With a shrug, she propped the fridge door open with an oversized bag of broccoli, and by the faint inside light searched the kitchen cupboards for a glass, plate, knife and fork. Smiling, she returned to the edible treasure and poured herself some milk. Then she reached for the pie.

A breeze swept through the kitchen, rattling the blinds. The back door slowly blew open.

Fiona froze. "Mrs. Glee must've forgotten to lock up," she told herself firmly. "Good thing I'm here to look after it."

She'd barely taken a step toward the door, when a dark figure bolted from behind, knocking her off balance.

"Hey!"

Fiona's outflung arm knocked the milk. The glass spun, whirling white stripes in all directions before crashing to the floor.

The pie flew across the kitchen, splattering globs of cherry onto the cupboards and streaking red across the tiles.

The prowler stopped and turned to face her.

The light from the fridge slid over his thin face and dark hair. His eyes narrowed and he stepped toward her. Fiona opened her mouth to scream.

The lights flicked on.

Uncle Harold, in striped pajamas, clutched a baseball bat. Swathed in bathrobes, Aunt Irene, Lisa and Scott hovered behind.

"Fiona! What are you doing?" Uncle Harold demanded.

Fiona shut her mouth. Something was definitely wrong. The prowler didn't run. He didn't do anything but wipe a red blob of pie off his chin.

"He...he broke in here!" Fiona pointed her finger at the stranger.

"Sorry, kid," the teenager said. "Didn't mean to scare you." He smiled at Fiona's aunt and uncle. "I just got home and saw there was someone creeping around in the kitchen – and no lights on. With all the break-ins, I figured I'd better check it out. So I used my key to let myself in."

"Thank you, Marcus," Uncle Harold said. With a tired grimace, he leaned the baseball bat against the counter. "This young lady is my wife's niece."

"I heard about you coming." Marcus grinned. "Why'd you pitch the pie at me, kid?"

Fiona's face burned. "I didn't! You knocked it out of my hands!"

"It looks like you played Frisbee with it," Lisa said. She stepped carefully around the gooey streaks. "You are such a disaster."

"Oh dear..." Aunt Irene quavered. "Look at this mess!"

Fiona followed the line of Aunt Irene's gaze. Milk flowed in a widening white puddle on the tiles. Sticky red cherries striped the floor and clung to the cupboards. The pie pan lay tilted against the dishwasher.

Fiona swallowed. "I...I'm sorry. I was hungry..."

"That's not surprising," Uncle Harold muttered. Marcus's smile thinned a little.

"I'm sorry. I'll clean it up," Fiona offered.

"Oh no..." Aunt Irene said. "I mean...oh my, we can't leave it like this until morning, can we?"

"Don't worry, Mrs. Vickers," Marcus said. "I'll mop up."

"Oh, Marcus, you're a dear!"

"No problem." Marcus went to the cupboard and took out a mop.

"I'm really sorry," Fiona said. "But I'd heard a noise from the study...I guess it was the breeze through the window..."

"I shut the all windows before I went to bed," Uncle Harold interrupted. Abruptly he left the kitchen.

"Irene!" he shouted a moment later. "Call the police! We've been robbed!"

Everyone rushed into Uncle Harold's study. Behind his desk, a framed antique map had been pulled aside revealing a wall safe. Its door hung open.

"My ring!" Aunt Irene cried. "Did you take it to the jewelers?"

Uncle Harold picked up the phone and punched emergency numbers. "No," he said tightly. Then, "Hello? This is Harold Vickers. Someone has broken into our home…"

Aunt Irene began to sob. "It was my mother's ring…Harold was going to have it cleaned…"

"Look!" Marcus pointed. The French windows were wide open.

"How'd he get past the alarms?" Lisa asked.

Marcus shrugged. "This guy's smart. He's not your run-of-the-mill housebreaker."

Uncle Harold gave the address of the house and hung up the phone. "I suggest we leave this room in case we disturb something that could help the police. Marcus, let's see what he did to the security system."

Aunt Irene huddled in an armchair. With Scott and Lisa beside her, Fiona watched from the living room window as blue and white police lights flashed toward them. When the squad car pulled in the driveway, Marcus and Uncle Harold returned from their inspection of the alarms.

Scott ran to the hallway and threw open the front door.

"Mr. Vickers," the senior officer said, "I'm Sergeant Reese."

"This way." Uncle Harold led them to the study.

Mrs. Glee, with sweat pants pulled over a nightgown, appeared a moment later at the front door. "Not a break-in!" she exclaimed.

Aunt Irene rushed toward her housekeeper, a soggy tissue in hand. "Oh, Mrs. Glee," she cried. "He took my mother's ring!"

Mrs. Glee awkwardly patted her employer's shoulder. "There now," she said with rough sympathy. "You just sit back down and I'll make some tea. You've had a bad shock."

"It's terrible!" Aunt Irene started crying again.

Fiona, Scott and Lisa looked at each other and slipped into the study. Marcus shot an appalled look at his weeping employer and followed.

Sergeant Reese was making notes in a little pad while the other policeman dusted silver-grey powder liberally across the door of the safe and the desk. The windowsill was already coated.

"Fingerprints!" Scott exclaimed. He crowded close to watch. "Can I help?"

"Sorry, son," the policeman said cheerfully.

"Scott, let him do his work," Lisa ordered. "How can he find out who did it if you're messing around?"

"I'm not!" Scott declared, but he stepped back.

Sergeant Reese turned to Fiona. "You heard the thief?"

"It was just a sound," Fiona told him. "I thought it was the breeze blowing Uncle Harold's files because I could feel the draft on my feet."

"So the window was ajar?" the policeman asked.

"Or maybe the kitchen door," Fiona said. "It blew open, so it couldn't have been shut tight."

"Everything was locked up when I went to bed," Uncle Harold said grimly. "And the alarm system was on."

"It's broke now," Marcus said. "I don't think I can fix it either."

"Same story at all the other break-ins," Reese said, shutting his notebook. "The burglar knows how to disable alarms and he knows this community."

"No prints." The other officer stood up. "Our thief's paid attention to his TV detective shows."

"It's that Lopez boy," Aunt Irene declared from the doorway. "Why don't you just arrest him? Everyone knows he's the thief!"

"That's a lie!" Lisa shouted.

"Lisa!" Aunt Irene gasped.

"Derek never stole anything in his life!" Lisa declared. "But Ginger Bocci keeps telling everybody he did, all out of spite!"

"That's a pretty serious thing to say about your friend," Sergeant Reese said. He put his notebook back in his pocket.

"She's not my friend." Lisa's eyes flashed.

"I guess not." Sergeant Reese turned to Uncle Harold. "We're about done here."

"What about the Lopez boy?" Uncle Harold ignored Lisa's look of fury. She plunked down in her father's chair. Grey powder puffed upward.

"We've questioned him."

"And?" Uncle Harold probed.

"We'll let you know if we make an arrest or locate your ring," Sergeant Reese said.

Just then Mrs. Glee stormed in. "My kitchen! They tore up my kitchen!"

Fiona felt her face heat up, but Mrs. Glee's eyes fell on the coating of fingerprint powder. "What's happened in here?"

"Fingerprints," Scott told her.

"It's all right, Mrs. Glee," Uncle Harold soothed. "The policemen are just doing their job. The kitchen was an accident."

"I'll look after the kitchen, Ma," Marcus said and eased his mother out of the room. Everyone but Lisa and Fiona followed.

"Why would Ginger tell lies about Derek?" Fiona asked.

Lisa rocked back in the chair. "Because she told everyone in eighth grade that she was going to the high school dance with him. But she didn't tell Derek. He turned her down flat in front of everybody."

"Ouch!" Fiona said.

Lisa's eyes gleamed. "He asked me, but I'm not allowed to date yet."

"You meet him every day. Isn't that like a date?"

Lisa's face whitened. "It's different. It doesn't mean anything."

Fiona shrugged. "Why does your mother let you hang out with him if she thinks he's a thief? My mom would kill me."

Lisa stood up and beat the powder off her bathrobe. "I don't tell her what she doesn't want to hear. You'd better not either." She walked out of the room.

Fiona stared after her. *Secrets*, she thought.

A few minutes later the policemen left. Uncle Harold ordered the kids to bed. Soon the lights were all switched off and the household settled again.

Fiona snuggled down in her blankets and stared at the ceiling. Everything was quiet – except for her growling stomach.

Chapter 6

Here Be Pirates

Fiona sat on the window seat, staring out at the water and distant mountains. Except for the muffled drumming of Lisa's shower, the room was quiet.

Today was Sunday. Tomorrow Mom would have the operation.

Fiona squeezed her eyes shut. She held out her arms and pulled them back as if she was giving Mom a hug. A glow of warmth spread over her, rising from her stomach. Yes, she was almost sure she'd gotten through.

Fiona opened her eyes. Lisa was watching.

"Is that some kind of ritual or something?" her cousin asked with raised eyebrows. Fiona's face flamed. Lisa sniffed the air and frowned. "And what's that smell?"

"How should I know?" Fiona said. "It's your house." She jumped up and went into the bathroom.

By the time she'd showered, Lisa had left.

Hearing the dull roar of the vacuum down the hall, Fiona hurried into her clothes. She wondered if Uncle Harold had heard anything from the police yet.

No one was at the breakfast table. Fiona helped herself to toast and walked across the lawn to the bluff where she could look all up and down the beach. On the far end of the Vickers' property, Marcus raked washed-up seaweed into neat piles.

In the other direction, she spotted Lisa by the sketching log. Today neither Derek nor the dog were there. Frowning, Fiona watched as Lisa paced back and forth.

"Guess he stood her up," Fiona murmured.

If Derek had broken into the house last night, it would take a lot of nerve to show up today. Fiona licked a last smear of butter from her thumb. Maybe Scott would go swimming with her.

An hour later, after a long swim with Scott, Fiona made her way upstairs. Mrs. Glee and her aunt had invaded her bedroom; Lisa stood in the middle of the room with her fists on her hips, and everyone was yelling.

Astounded by the noise, Fiona stared from the threshold.

"I don't care if you did just vacuum," Lisa insisted. "My room smells!"

"I don't have to take this," Mrs. Glee declared. "I come in on my day off to help clean up after last night. But does anybody appreciate it? No!"

"Oh, dear...you know I'm very grateful..." Aunt Irene fluttered.

The housekeeper kept right on talking. "Mrs. V, if you aren't satisfied with my work, I can go. That Mrs. Bocci down the beach has asked me twice to come work for her. But I said no, Mrs. V treats me good!"

"She probably didn't offer you as much money," Lisa snapped.

"Oh Lisa, don't say such things," Aunt Irene gasped. "She doesn't mean it, Mrs. Glee. Lisa's just...she's high-strung..."

"Spoiled, if you ask me," Mrs. Glee muttered.

"Mother!" Lisa stomped her foot. "This room stinks!"

Fiona sniffed. There was a noticeably sour odor in the air. Her aunt must've smelt it too, because her eyebrows rose in distaste and she blinked rapidly.

"Perhaps it's a little musty," she offered. "If we air the room..."

"It shouldn't *be* musty," Lisa ground out.

Mrs. Glee sniffed the air like a hound, and then stalked across the room towards Fiona's bed. Fiona's stomach lurched.

The housekeeper leaned over and lifted the edge of the bedspread. The odor of mildew and rotting seaweed wafted upwards.

"My clothes," Fiona squeaked. Her jeans and t-shirt, soaked in seawater from the horrible night on the beach, had been heaped under the bed for two very warm days.

Mrs. Glee fished them out. They fabric had crusted into a stiff, twisted ball. Black mildew stains dotted the *Save the Whales* logo on the t-shirt.

"I'm sorry," Fiona faltered. "I didn't see a hamper...and...and I forgot about them...."

Holding the offending bundle like a rat with rigor mortis, Mrs. Glee stomped from the room. Lisa groaned and threw herself on her bed.

"I'm sorry, Aunt Irene," Fiona repeated miserably.

"Yes, dear, well..." Her aunt frowned. "Fiona I have to say I'm quite angry over this. I asked you to try and adjust to our family, and after last night...and now this on the rug... well...who knows if the smell will come out... but perhaps when it dries.... Oh, dear.... Mrs. Glee!" She hurried out after the housekeeper.

"Lisa," Fiona tried again, "I'm sorry. But it's partly your fault for dumping me on the beach."

Lisa rolled over, eyes blazing. "Oh yeah, sure. And I put your filthy, wet clothes under the bed?"

"That was a mistake."

"You're a mistake!" Lisa got up and stormed out of the room.

Fiona sank down onto her bed, but the nose-catching mildew smell rose upward. Giving up, she went downstairs. Through the glass doors, she spotted Lisa sitting on a patio chair, jabbing numbers into her phone.

Probably going to tell all her snobby friends about her horrible cousin, Fiona thought.

Blinking hard, she veered right to slip out the pool's sliding glass doors. To one side, Bruce, the gardener, crawled on his hands and knees by the study window. Weird. There was no garden there, only a couple of neatly trimmed bushes. Maybe he was after some stray weeds.

Fiona shrugged – why should she care what Bruce did? Before he could notice her, she sprinted toward the boathouse where steps led down to the beach.

The boathouse rose two stories high. Fiona raced past the white painted top section where the Glees lived. It looked like a storybook cottage with its red and white geraniums growing in black window boxes.

When she reached the door of the bottom section – the actual boathouse – Fiona slowed down. She gave the boathouse door a little push. It squealed on rusty hinges.

Inside was room for two or three big boats but only a single motor boat bobbed in the water. Gas cans, ropes, water skis, and other boating paraphernalia had been stacked on wooden shelves against the walls. A kind of U-shaped boardwalk surrounded the open water. There was no sign of anyone.

Fiona pushed the door shut, and sat down at the end of the dock, dangling her feet. The tide was out, so the water was about four feet below the soles of her shoes.

"Watcha doin', kid?"

Fiona twisted around. Marcus sauntered down the steps toward her, a fishing pole in one hand and a black plastic tackle box in the other.

"I'm going out fishing," he said. "Want to come along?"

After the humiliation of last night's cherry pie episode, the idea of going fishing with Marcus made Fiona want to squirm.

"No, thanks. I have to write a letter to my mother."

Marcus shrugged. "Suit yourself."

He went into the boathouse. A moment later, the ocean-front doors banged open, a motor roared, and the boat shot out over the water.

Before long, the drone of the motor faded away. Fiona wished she could talk to her mom or even Jimmy. But she couldn't upset her mother, and Fiona knew what her brother would say.

"What's your problem?" he'd demand. *"I told you. Pay her back double!"*

"It's not that easy," Fiona said aloud. Restlessly, she stood up and headed back toward the house.

Now Aunt Irene was on the patio talking on her phone to someone about her party next Thursday. Fiona could see Mrs. Glee through the kitchen window. Bruce was glumly whacking away at the bushes again.

Circling the house, Fiona went in the front door. Uncle Harold was just coming down the stairs.

He looked intently at his niece. "I'm going into Seattle, to work in my office for a few hours. I can get some quiet on a Sunday. Do you want to come along?"

Surprised, Fiona realized Uncle Harold was trying to be nice.

"Thank you." She made herself smile. "But I have to write a postcard to my mom."

Uncle Harold looked relieved, but added, "You could do that in my office...but I suppose it wouldn't be very exciting." He jingled his keys uncomfortably in his pocket. "There are pens, paper, and such in my desk in the study. You could be private there."

This time, Fiona smiled for real. "Thanks, Uncle Harold." She reached up and kissed him on the cheek.

He blushed. "Yes, well. I'll see you at dinner... such as it is." Humming to himself, he left.

Fiona went upstairs for a postcard, but then hesitated by the door. Lisa was seated on the window seat, looking out over the water. Her dangling sketch pad showed a half-finished drawing of a soaring great blue heron carrying a jeweled bracelet in its beak.

Fiona took a deep breath. "Lisa, we have to talk."

"No, thanks."

"What have I done to you?" Fiona demanded.

Lisa flipped her sketchpad shut. "You made up to Ginger Bocci for one..."

"I did not!"

"And," Lisa continued, "every time I turn around, you're spying on me."

"Get real, Lisa. I don't care about your little secrets."

"I don't want you here!" Her cousin stood up. "And somehow, I'm going to make my mother send you home."

"I can't go home," Fiona retorted. "My mom needs to rest and be quiet."

Lisa's eyes flickered. "I'm sorry she's sick and I can see why she wants you out of her hair. But it's not my problem." She walked out.

Fiona stood in the middle of the floor, clenching and unclenching her teeth, so angry she was shaking. She hated Lisa!

No way she was going to let her cousin bully her out of the house. If staying at Aunt Irene's was the best Fiona could do to help her mom get better, then that's what she'd do – no matter what!

Fiona got a postcard and went downstairs to Uncle Harold's study.

The mess from last night had been whisked away. Once again, the antique map of the San Juan Islands hung behind the desk, hiding the safe. The fingerprint powder had been cleaned from the windowsill, paneling and shelves of books. The room smelled of polish and leather.

Fiona sat in Uncle Harold's chair, laid the postcard exactly in the center of the desk, and opened the top drawer. Inside, each in its own wooden tray, lay pens and pencils, paper clips, and a roll of stamps.

She chose a pen, slid the drawer shut, then after a moment's thought, wrote:

Pirates, Prowlers, and Cherry Pie   69

Dear Mom,

Hi! How are you feeling? By the time you get this, you'll have had your operation. I hope it didn't hurt too much and they give you lots of ice cream.

I'm having a great time. I went with Lisa to a bonfire on the beach Friday night. I've been swimming in the pool a lot too. It's so super gorgeous here that I keep trying to send you pictures of it in your mind. In case they don't get there, the picture on the front of this postcard is almost as pretty.

Love, Fiona xoxoxoxoxoxoxox

There was hardly enough room for the hugs and kisses, but Fiona ran them over to the address section. She filled that in, borrowed one of Uncle Harold's stamps, and sat back.

Lisa had made it clear she would try to get rid of her cousin, no matter what.

Fiona spun slowly in the big chair.

Maybe Jimmy was right. Pay her back double. Make sure Lisa knew that giving Fiona a bad time would cause worse trouble for herself.

She needed a plan, Fiona decided. Something incredible. Something brilliant. Something that would make Lisa treat her with respect.

But what?

With a shove of her foot Fiona spun the chair around and around. This time it stopped facing the antique map. A cloud-shaped god puffed a sailing ship across the lower corner. Curly-cued letters spelled out – *Here be Pirates 1890*.

"Too bad I can't get those nasty guys after Lisa," Fiona mused.

And then the truly brilliant idea unfolded in her mind. Even Jimmy would be impressed.

Pirates *would* pay Lisa back.

Susan Brown

Chapter 7

Revenge Is...Smelly

Fiona squinted her eyes against the sun.

It was hot on the beach. Swarms of flies rose from stinky heaps of rotting seaweed. Down here, between the big houses and the public docks, nobody raked the beach clean like Marcus did at Vickers Villa.

An old tide wall, made of rotting, upright timbers crowded close to the bluff. At one end the timbers had reeled over, but they were still attached to each other by steel cables so they didn't completely fall.

Fiona walked over and peered behind the wall.

Puddles of oily water snaked between the timbers and the bluff. Tangled plants leaned against the wood, yearning upward toward the light. Fiona wrinkled her nose. It smelled like a greenhouse, gas station and swamp all mixed together.

"Disgusting," she said with a smile.

Ancient wet logs lay jumbled end to end, over the puddles. Jumping onto the first, she held her arms out for balance and walked along.

The air dropped about ten degrees – like a cave.

Counting her steps, Fiona ran from one log to the next. At step fifty-two, her foot slipped on a patch of moss.

She fell, straddling the log. Her right foot went up to the ankle in black, oozy mud. Her hand scraped the slithery, wet timbers.

"Oh, *yuck!*"

Fiona snatched back her hand and yanked up her foot. A stench like rotten eggs came with it. Despite gagging a little, Fiona smiled. No way Lisa, with her perfect hair and designer jeans, would make it.

Revenge is a smelly undertaking.

With a deep breath, Fiona kept going. *One hundred and fourteen feet.* She leapt off the last log into the sunlight and took a deep breath, then carefully wrote in her notepad:

Tide wall – 114

What next?

It was too easy to just send Lisa back along the beach. A faint rabbit path led up the crumbly side of the bluff. Shoving the pad in her pocket, Fiona started climbing.

Using protruding roots for handholds, barely avoiding a patch of stinging nettles, and almost sliding down when a rock broke loose under her foot, she made it to the top. Her hands stung and she was streaked with dust and grime.

Revenge is a dirty game.

Panting, Fiona sat on the edge and wrote in her notebook:

Dead Man's Cliff – 20

She was only a few feet from the road. Across it lay the field where Scott had caught a snake. Fiona didn't like snakes, but she'd bet that Lisa hated them even more.

Counting as she went, Fiona got up and trotted across the road to the edge of the field. A huge old tree trunk stood on the far side. Perfect.

"*...twenty-six, twenty-seven...*"

Fiona swiped at the spitbug clumps sticking to her legs and then had to wipe the goo from her fingers. This whole field seemed to be a spitbug colony.

At fifty-eight, a very small snake slid through the grass in front of her.

Fiona took a deep breath and did not scream. At least not until she felt six tiny prickles on her hand.

"Aargh!!!"

Shrieking, she jumped back. A swallowtail butterfly fluttered away. Using her sleeve, Fiona wiped her forehead.

Revenge is a nerve-wracking business.

At the tree trunk, Fiona wrote in her notebook:

Blasted Tree – 86

Ahead stood the blackberry and salmonberry thickets. Fiona paced her way toward them.

Brambles – 21

There was no way through. She scouted around until she found a passage, almost a tunnel, through a salmonberry tangle.

Right – 19
Left ...

Fiona stopped. She could see spider webs. Large, criss-crossing, layers of spider webs. She poked one with a stalk of grass. The web quivered and then a huge brown spider skittered down the strands.

Fiona leaped back.

No way. Not ever. Not in a hundred years. There were at least a million of the little arachnids in there. Maybe two million.

Fiona loped back to the road and circled the bushes from the other side. She'd guess the distance. Besides, perfect Lisa would never make it this far. Not a chance.

Revenge is a creepy experience.

She wrote in her notebook:

Left – 26

Then she angled back across the field, heading for the public docks. After scaling a heap of discarded tires, rags, old sinks and car parts, she ran down the other side to the beach.

Waves lapped over sand and sloshed against tarry pylons that supported the huge pier. Thumps echoed underneath as people unloaded cargo at the end. About twenty motor boats were tied to a criss-cross of floating docks nearby.

Fiona crouched to peer under the main pier where the shore sloped down. Sun never reached under here. The wet sand was littered with flotsam – rotten fish, plastic bottles, bits of driftwood, rank seaweed....

Revenge is a disgusting sight.
Fiona wrote in her notebook:

Northeast – 215
North – 8
Here be the Treasure!!!

Fiona grinned with pride. This treasure hunt would pay back Lisa, double...triple...quadruple!!!

Phase One was finished. She'd better get going with *Phase Two*.

Back at the house, Fiona came in through the kitchen door. Mrs. Glee turned from the stove and stared.

"You look a fright," she told Fiona. "And you smell like rotten fish."

"Thanks!" Fiona stomped past her and upstairs. "Better than acting like one," she muttered.

The shower felt wonderful. Grudgingly, she admitted that Mrs. Glee might have been correct about the odor. The shoe that had gone into the slime puddle still had a dead fish smell. Fiona tossed it into the shower and turned the water on full blast until the mud washed away.

She ran down to lunch barefoot. No one noticed. Scott's place was empty and his plate held a sandwich crust. Lisa was arguing with her mom.

"But I have to go into town this afternoon," Lisa insisted. "It's important."

Fiona took a tuna sandwich from the platter and bit in.

"Now dear, you know you can invite your friends over here. I don't feel safe with all the strangers wandering around town...."

"They're called tourists," Lisa snapped.

"We don't know who they are. And after these burglaries...."

Fiona thought quickly. "I need to mail a postcard to my mom. Lisa and I could go in together."

"Oh dear...I'm not sure." Aunt Irene's forehead wrinkled into a slight frown. "But then I suppose if you go, too.... Perhaps you could stop at the florists and give them my order for the party. Mickey does such nice arrangements...."

"I'm not taking her!" Lisa insisted. "She's a walking disaster! After last night, she should've been grounded for life!"

"Lisa, last night is a closed issue," her mother said. "Besides, Fiona probably frightened off that burglar."

"Maybe she let him in!"

"Lisa! Enough! I won't allow you to go into town alone." Aunt Irene put her napkin beside her plate and stood up. "And I want you two to stay together."

She left.

Lisa threw her napkin on the table. "I told you I wasn't going to baby-sit you!"

Fiona took the last bite of her sandwich and licked a dab of mayonnaise off her thumb.

"I think you've got it backwards, Lisa. Your mom won't let *you* go without *me*." She got up. "I've got a couple of things to do. I'll meet you around two."

Chuckling gleefully, Fiona ducked into Uncle Harold's study. He had said she could use his paper. Fiona opened the desk drawers until she found what she wanted – a big sheet of heavy white paper.

Standing on the far side of the desk so she could look directly at the map, Fiona sketched the outline. Some of the lines were a little too far one way or the other, but Fiona thought it would fool her cousin.

However, she was fairly sure, pirates didn't use #2 pencils. The outline had to be drawn with good black ink. The kind artists use....

Fiona left the study and hurried upstairs. Lisa had a whole drawer full of art supplies, including black drawing ink. Fiona took the ink, decided against a calligraphy pen, added her pocket knife to the supplies, and then detoured into the kitchen for a packet of matches.

Avoiding everyone, Fiona slipped out of the house and ran down to the beach.

It took several minutes to find two seagull feathers that Marcus hadn't raked up. The feather parts were bedraggled, but the quills were just fine. Sitting in the warm sand out of sight of the house, Fiona set to work.

Her attempts to sharpen the feather into a pen ruined the first quill. But then she got the knack. The tip of the second feather looked just like pictures of pens she'd seen in her history books.

Dipping the quill into the ink, Fiona retraced the pencil lines with scratchy black ink strokes. Blobs of ink dripped onto the sand and stained her fingers.

A puff of wind blew sand across the paper. She shook it off and dipped her quill pen again.

It took almost an hour of concentrated effort to get the map outlines right, trace a dotted trail, and print in the directions.

Here Be Treasure...

Fiona scratched an *X* then sat back to admire her work.

She'd drawn the trail carefully – behind the tide wall, up the side of the bluff, across the spitbug field, through the spidery brambles, over the rubbish by the public dock, then down underneath.

It was a smelly, dirty, nerve-wracking, creepy, disgusting revenge. Jimmy would be impressed.

But the map looked too clean and new. Fiona tried rubbing it with a handful of sand to roughen the smooth look. A few specks of tar stuck to the paper.

Better, but not old looking.

Using one of the matches, Fiona waved a flame back and forth about an inch below the map. The paper smoked then slowly tinged brown.

"Ouch!" Fiona dropped the match stub and sucked her finger.

Scooping damp sand over the map, she counted to a hundred. When she dug it up again, the black lines had bled and the brittle edges had softened.

It was a perfect pirate's treasure map.

As she headed up to the house with the map hidden under her shirt, Fiona felt a lot like a pirate herself.

Chapter 8

Meet Your Doom

Lisa walked fast on the road to town, making sure she stayed a little ahead of her cousin. Fiona only smiled and patted the hard square of folded paper in her pocket.

Just before they reached the main street, Lisa slowed and turned toward Fiona.

"Like I told you before, I have some private things to do," she said. "As soon as we get to town, you can get lost."

"Count on it," Fiona retorted. "But if we go back separately your mother will know we didn't do what she said."

Lisa bit her lip. "All right. We can meet at the thrift shop in an hour. Will that satisfy you?"

Fiona shrugged.

Lisa scowled but added, "They have a lot of cool things there – old clothes and books and stuff – so you can look around if I'm a little late."

"No problem," Fiona said. Exactly what was Lisa up to that she needed privacy so badly? It might be worth her while to check it out...not that she didn't trust her cousin. Like not at all.

They walked up the last hill overlooking the Saratoga Passage, past the library and pharmacy and into town. Lisa kept peering down the side streets as if looking for something. Fiona pretended she didn't notice. Main Street was lined with cars. Local people, summer residents and tourists wandered in and out of the shops.

At the beginning of the street, the sidewalk bulged into an overlook of the Passage. Fiona ran to the steel railing and draped her arm around a life-size, sun-warm statue of a boy and his dog looking out over the sea. A few sailboats skimmed the water below. The mainland rose dusky green beyond them.

"I've got to go," Lisa said. "Will you order mom's flowers?"

Fiona dropped her arm and turned. "Okay. Where's the florist's?"

"On the next block, beside the ice cream parlor. Meet you at four o'clock?"

Fiona nodded agreement but watched as her cousin crossed the road and disappeared down a narrow walkway to the next street.

Exactly what was Lisa doing that was so secret and important?

Trying to look casual, Fiona loitered along the sidewalk trying to keep her cousin in view. She dropped her postcard into a mailbox, and stood behind it, watching Lisa hesitate, and then run up the steps and disappear into a square, cement building.

Fiona followed, then stopped abruptly. Lisa had gone into the police station. Did she know something about the robberies?

Feeling like she was somehow trespassing into Lisa's life, Fiona did an about-face and hurried back toward the main part of town, past antique shops and boutiques until she reached the flower shop. Mickey took the order, smiled with satisfaction and wished Fiona a good day.

Still feeling yucky about spying on her cousin, Fiona immediately headed to the Ice Creamery.

Several kids from the Friday Night Club, including Tiffany and Ginger Bocci, sat at the scattered tables.

"Hi!" Fiona said.

"Oh, hi," Ginger replied, but didn't turn away from her friends. Tiffany ignored her. Fiona stared at the menu posted on the wall. Her face flamed red. This trip into town was not going well at all.

"Can I help you?" the man behind the counter asked.

"I...uh, I'll have an ice cream bar, please." She pushed her money over the counter. The man took the dessert out of the freezer and handed it to her.

"Thanks."

"Hey...your name's Fiona, isn't it?" Ginger asked suddenly.

"Yes." Fiona concentrated on unwrapping the ice cream.

"Where's your cousin?"

Fiona felt her face get even hotter as she crumpled the wrapper and tossed it into the garbage. "I'm not her baby-sitter."

Ginger stuck out the tip of her pink tongue to lick her cone. She smiled. "So what's Lisa got to say about Derek robbing her, too?"

Fiona peeled off a piece of chocolate and popped it in her mouth. "Seeing as she doesn't think he did it, she hasn't said anything."

Ginger rolled her eyes. "Even Lisa can't be that dense. They've arrested him!"

"Are you sure? When?" Fiona's breathing quickened.

"Last night," Tiffany said. "Right after they were at your place."

"But there were no clues...not even fingerprints!" Fiona insisted.

"Maybe not at the Vickers', but the cops found a school jacket at the break-in Friday night," Ginger said. "Once they proved it was Derek's, all they had to do was find the creep."

"I'm glad they got him," one of the boys said.

"Me too," Tiffany agreed. "I thought he was nice. I can't believe he'd rob us. I mean, we've been friends since we were little. I keep wondering if he came into my room while I was asleep."

"Oh, yuck," one of the other girls exclaimed and shivered.

"Derek's a jerk," Ginger declared. "I hope the judge really nails him."

Fiona left, butterflies running riot in her stomach. She ate some more of the chocolate coating and licked the drips. She'd almost believed Lisa when she declared Derek was innocent. But if the police had found his jacket at the scene of a robbery....

Fiona scowled. Too bad for Derek. And too bad for Lisa, because Fiona still owed her payback.

She went down to the shore. The tide was just going out, leaving this part of the beach too smooshy to walk on. Fiona checked her watch. Three-thirty. Still too early to meet Lisa.

Instead she walked along by the ten-foot cement tide wall. Except for the crumbling cement steps, it was as if the town above didn't exist.

She touched her jeans pocket. It was still hard with the folded pirate map. Somehow she had to find a way to slip it to her cousin. At a quarter to four, Fiona speeded up, heading toward a stairwell.

Then she heard voices – angry ones. There was something familiar about them. Fiona hesitated then rechecked her watch. Resolutely she kept going.

In the stairwell, the tops of two men's heads rose above the cement wall. One wore a police cap. The other had sandy hair – Sergeant Reese and Bruce Lansford.

"I'm warning you...get off my back!" Bruce snarled.

"Not a chance," Sergeant Reese snapped. "I've caught my burglar, Lansford. And I'll catch any opportunist who decides to pick up where that kid left off. I want you out of my town."

"So arrest me," Bruce mocked. Turning to go, he caught sight of Fiona. They both froze.

"Um...hi!" Fiona said. "I uh...have to go...." She darted past him and Sergeant Reese and tore up the steps toward town.

"Hey!" the policeman called. Fiona kept going. She hadn't done anything wrong...had she?

Inside the *Good Cheer Thrift Shop*, Fiona hurried past the crowded racks of clothes, household items and used toys, heading instead for the books. Rows and rows of books, mostly marked at a dollar or less, all crammed on yellow painted shelves.

"All right!" she breathed.

There were hundreds of paperbacks and a lot of ragged hardcovers with the titles printed in worn gold letters.

Head cocked to the side, Fiona read through the rows of packed titles. Cookbooks... Backpacking...World War II Fighter Planes... Psychology... and then she saw it: *Whalers, Pioneers, and Pirates: A Selective History of the Northwest*.

"Lisa, prepare to meet your doom!" The book was full of sketches of the coastline, old ships, and spouting whales.

She glanced across the store. Lisa had come in and was standing by the entrance. When her cousin spotted her, Fiona waved.

Lisa lifted her hand and went over to a rack of scarves.

Fiona stepped behind the bookshelves, out

of her cousin's view, and examined the binding. Perfect! The paper lining had worn loose in a couple of places. Gently, Fiona pushed her finger under the paper. It pulled partly away from the cover, leaving a tight pocket.

She slid the folded map between the lining and cover, then stood on tiptoes to look over the shelf. Lisa had moved her attention to kitchen ware and was moodily staring at a stack of mixing bowls.

Fiona picked out two paperbacks and then went to the cash register.

An elderly woman in a vibrantly pink floral blouse came over to wait on her. "May I help you, dear?"

"I'd like to get these please." Fiona laid the books and a five dollar bill on the counter. The old woman picked up the hardcover book.

"My," she said. "This one's a real antique. Do you collect books?"

Lisa walked over. Apparently she'd decided against the mixing bowls.

"Not really," Fiona said. "My cousin likes to draw whales and the ocean. This has neat pictures."

Lisa took the book and examined it. "Cool," she said. "I'll get it."

"I was going to buy it for you," Fiona said firmly. "To help fix our relationship."

"I'll pay for it," Lisa said, handing a ten dollar bill to the sales lady. With an apologetic look at Fiona, the woman took the money and then slowly counted out change. She repeated the process for Fiona's paperbacks.

In silence, the two girls walked back to the house. Lisa kept a little ahead, as if she didn't even want to be on the same road with her cousin.

Fiona only smiled. She couldn't wait until Lisa found the map!

Susan Brown

Chapter 9

Rocky Road

It was nearly 5pm before Lisa and Fiona got back home. Lisa went upstairs. The bedroom door slammed.

Fiona decided to take a look at the control box for the security system. She found Marcus there already, surrounded by snips of wire, pliers and screwdrivers.

"Any luck?" she asked.

Marcus wiped his forehead on his sleeve. "Nah. It's been really trashed. It's the same kind as all the security systems around here." He pointed a screwdriver in the general direction of the homes lining the bluff. "Really basic."

"You mean easy to break into?"

"Just about any idiot could do it."

"I couldn't," Fiona protested.

"Guess you're not an idiot, then!" Marcus grinned at her.

Fiona laughed and, with a wave, went hunting for Scott. She found him in the family room sitting cross-legged in front of a video game. His eyes didn't move from the screen; his hand maneuvered the joystick so fast it appeared wired to his brain.

"Want to go swimming?" Fiona asked.

No answer.

"Scott! Do you want to go swimming?" Fiona shouted.

He turned his head slightly. "What?...Oh, no!"

Computer music blared. Scott's shoulders slumped.

"You made me die," he told her bitterly. "I bet Michael I'd get to the tenth level this weekend."

The screen flashed a request for a new game. Fiona thought fast. "Maybe a swim will relax you so you can play even better."

"Maybe." He switched off the machine. "This game sucks anyway. Michael's got the new version and it has way better graphics."

"What does that do?"

"The blood and guts look really gory when you die." Scott grinned.

Fiona decided she could live without new graphics.

Scott was diving for a stone and Fiona was floating on her back, letting the wavelets lap over her chin when Aunt Irene hurried in holding up her phone.

"Fiona.... It's your mother!"

"What?" Fiona swallowed a mouthful, but coughing and gagging she splashed hurriedly to the side of the pool.

She was hardly out of the water before she had the phone to her ear. "Mom! How are you? I thought Dad would phone."

"I'm fine, sweetie," Fiona's mom said. "Just wanted to say hi. I'll probably be too groggy after the operation tomorrow."

Fiona felt like she had a marshmallow stuck in her windpipe. Sticky. Hard to talk. "Are you scared?"

Her mom hesitated. "Kind of," she said. "But it'll be fine. Send me good thoughts."

"All morning, from the minute I wake up. I've been concentrating on orcas – you know, killer whales."

"They're my favorites." There was a clattering noise in the background. "What... oh..." mom said. "Okay...Fiona, sweetie, I have to go. My doctor's here to tell me about the operation. I love you, baby."

"I love you, too, Mom."

The phone clicked. Fiona handed it to her aunt and turned and dove back into the pool. You can't cry under water.

That night Fiona dreamed.

She dreamed that a pirate ship came sailing toward the dock where Mom waited. Fiona ran down the boathouse steps, but they grew longer and twistier and her feet got heavier and heavier. Snakes and spiders slithered by. Jungle vines tangled up and over the steps.

Fiona cried out. Mom didn't seem to hear. The pirate ship sailed closer and closer. And then it was so close a pirate leaned over and scooped her up.

Mom! With a cry, Fiona woke up.

Everything was dark. Across the room, Lisa breathed peacefully. Fiona gasped for breath. She was sweating, as though she really had run down all those stairs.

Good thoughts, Fiona ordered herself. *Good thoughts....*

She got out of bed and curled up on the window seat. The moonlight pulled shrubs' outlines into monster shapes. It swirled distant waves into sea serpents and shipwrecks.

Fiona shut her eyes and tried to breathe slowly.

Don't be dumb, she told herself. *Those shapes out there are buoys and fishing boats. There's nothing scary. Nothing at all.*

She'd sit where she was all night...sending good thoughts to Mom...keeping watch for pirate ships....

She slipped back to sleep, still leaning against the window.

Lisa had already gotten up and left. Fiona moved slowly, trying to stretch out her stiff muscles. A blanket slipped off her shoulders. Lisa must've covered her.

The book about pirates still lay on the desk. Trailing the blanket, Fiona checked for the map – it was still wedged tightly under the binding. Just as well. She couldn't cope with revenge today.

The clock read 7:15. Mom's operation was scheduled for 7:30.

Fiona dropped the blanket on the bed and pulled on her clothes.

Downstairs, she helped herself to a pear then left the house. Avoiding everyone, she went down the steps to the beach.

In the shallows, a great blue heron hunted for fish. Every few minutes, its neck curled back into a question mark, then its long, sharp beak stabbed into the water.

Fiona thought the picture towards her mom in case she dreamed under the anesthesia.

A motorboat with a couple of fishermen chugged by. The heron spread huge wings, lurched into the air and, with a screech, flew away.

Picking a sunny spot, Fiona sat down to absorb the scene before her – waving blue water with a background of misty purple mountains. After she'd thought that toward her mom too, she took out the pear and slowly ate it.

She didn't want to think about her mom lying in the hospital, so she concentrated on the robberies and what Ginger and Tiffany had said.

She should be glad the police had caught the thief – the idea that he'd been in the very next room the other night was extremely creepy.

Fiona crunched another mouthful of pear. Somehow, though, Derek still didn't look like her idea of a robber.

But Sergeant Reese had evidence. Fiona shivered, remembering his conversation with Bruce. Did he think Bruce was planning to rob houses too? The guy seemed weird enough.

Fiona nibbled the last of the pear.

It seemed very careless of Derek to lose his jacket at a break-in, especially as no clues at all had been left at the other burglaries. She could've understood something small being dropped, like a key or a comb or even a wallet.

But a whole jacket?

Fiona tossed the core. Sea gulls and crows came wheeling and squawking through the sky, and dove for it. Fiona laughed, shut her eyes and worked on sending that picture to her mother too.

In the background, a motorboat roared, whipping the shoreline into a slapping wash.

Fiona's eyes flew open.

Marcus stood at the wheel of the family's motorboat, wind streaming through his dark hair, speeding toward the boathouse.

Fiona held her breath. But just when it looked like he'd crash for sure, the boy throttled down and cut the motor. The boat drifted rather quickly through the open doors.

Careless, Fiona thought. Maybe all teenage boys are careless.

It must be almost time for Dad to call. Forgetting everything else, Fiona jumped up, shook the pins and needles from her legs and ran back up the wooden steps. She'd find somewhere quiet and private to wait.

"Hi, kid!" Marcus called from the door of the boathouse.

Fiona waved but didn't stop. Once inside the bedroom, she unplugged her phone from the charger and settled on the window seat. And waited.

It didn't ring.

Fiona got up and paced, back and forth, back and forth. The room started to feel too closed in, so she went slowly downstairs to the patio, sat in one of the wrought iron chairs and waited...and waited...and waited. Lisa came out and paused by the table.

"Heard from your Dad yet?"

Fiona shook her head.

"It'll be fine," Lisa said. "Don't worry."

"Sure," Fiona answered. But she thought, *how could she know?*

When lunch was served, Fiona couldn't even look at the grilled cheese sandwiches and pea soup. Mumbling "Excuse me..." she pushed away from the table.

"Oh dear," Fiona heard Aunt Irene say through the door. "It's taking such a long time. I hope nothing's gone wrong."

"Nothing's wrong," Lisa insisted. "Don't say that."

Fiona ran down the lawn to the edge of the bluff, and sat holding her knees, staring out at the waves.

When her phone finally did ring, she'd been concentrating so hard on listening, she thought at first she'd imagined it.

"Daddy?" she cried into the phone.

"Everything's fine, Funny-face." Her dad's voice was tired and happy. "The operation went even better than the doctors hoped."

Fiona started crying, and didn't even care. "Can I talk to Mom?"

Her dad laughed. "Not today. She's still half out from the anesthesia. It'll probably be a day or so before she's strong enough to call you. Everything going okay?"

"Yes. Fine."

"Good. I'd better call Jimmy now. Be good, Funny-face."

"I will," Fiona promised. "Bye."

Fiona pressed the turn-off switch. Aunt Irene's stood a few feet away, her make-up smeared around her eyes as though she'd been crying too.

Fiona grinned. "Mom's okay."

Aunt Irene smiled back. "I'm so happy. So relieved...what do you say we have some ice cream?"

"Great. I'm starving."

They were each on their second helping of Rocky Road when Lisa came back up from the beach.

"My mom's okay!" Fiona sang out.

Lisa grinned. "Great. That's really great news, Fiona."

Fiona dug her spoon into the ice cream. "Want some ice cream? We're celebrating."

"It's Rocky Road," Aunt Irene added.

"Ice cream? No." Lisa took a breath. "Mom, if I needed quite a bit of money for something really important, would you give it to me?"

Aunt Irene eyed her daughter. "Well, dear...I don't know. I mean if it were really important... and you know that your father likes to keep a strict...What could you need money for?"

Lisa bit her lip. "Never mind. I'll ask Dad when he gets home."

"Are you sure you wouldn't like some ice cream?"

"I said no!" Lisa flung out of the room.

Aunt Irene sadly stirred her ice cream. She sighed. "Lisa *is* a teenager," she told Fiona.

Lisa's a brat, Fiona thought.

As soon as she was finished, Fiona went upstairs to find her cousin. Lisa was sitting on the window seat, staring out at the water.

"Want to go swimming?" Fiona asked.

"I want to be alone! Can't you understand that?" Lisa jumped up and ran from the room.

"Suit yourself," Fiona said to the empty room. With a shrug she went hunting for Scott and spent the rest of the afternoon learning the fine points of playing his newest video game.

"Me and Michael played it the whole spring vacation," Scott confided. "And when his mom said we had to stop, we came over here."

"Didn't your eyeballs rot?"

Scott rolled his eyes back in his head and pretended to die. It was a long, noisy process.

The corpse revived four times before jerking into immobility.

That night, Fiona found herself yawning over dinner even though she was starving. Mrs. Glee had the afternoon off, so Aunt Irene fixed the meal. It wasn't very elegant – hamburgers, canned baked beans and salad – but it was the best meal Fiona'd had since she came.

Aunt Irene apologized at least seven times for the food not being very good, but no one answered. They were all too busy eating. Except Lisa. She stared at her plate and curtly refused her mom's offer of salad.

Later, after two helpings of cake, Fiona dragged herself up to bed. She was so tired she could hardly keep her eyes open.

She'd just pulled the covers up when she heard Lisa yelling downstairs...then Uncle Harold shouting back. Whatever was going on, Fiona didn't want any part of it. She was too tired. With a sigh, she burrowed down and pulled the blankets over her head.

When Lisa stormed into the room a few minutes later, Fiona stayed under cover.

Stomp, stomp, stomp....

Fiona lifted up the edge of the blanket nest and watched Lisa pace the floor. Back and forth...back and forth.

Furiously, her cousin swung clenched fists

at the air. *"It's not fair! I hate them...It just isn't fair!"*

Reluctantly awake, Fiona kept watching.

Lisa sat on the bed and started to get undressed. She pulled off her left shoe.

"How can they be so prejudiced!" Lisa winged the shoe across the room.

Thump! It hit the door.

"I'll show them!"

Thump! The right shoe hit the wall.

"I'll get it myself!"

Fiona burrowed further into her blankets. Lisa threw herself back onto the bed with a loud grunt. As Fiona finally drifted off to sleep, she distantly heard Lisa's reading light click on.

Chapter 10

Spitbugs and Spiders

Sunlight streamed in the window and danced over Fiona's eyelids. The soft click of the bedroom door being closed pulled her fully awake. Reluctantly, she gazed blearily across the room. Her cousin's bed was empty.

Fiona stretched and yawned. With a languid kick she freed her feet from the knot of blankets, sat up, and glanced over at the open book.

The binding had been ripped open – the map was gone!

Lisa had taken the bait!

Fiona bounded out of bed and ran to the window. Map fluttering in hand, Lisa ran down the boathouse steps and out of sight.

"Yes!" Fiona raced to pull on jeans and a t-shirt. Without bothering to lace her sneakers, she tore downstairs and out of the house. She wasn't going to miss a minute of her payback.

Like a pirate, she stood at the top of the bluff and surveyed the beach. Below, Lisa ran along the shore toward the tide wall.

Fiona raced to the road and jogged in the direction of town. Where the road overlooked the Saratoga Passage, she jumped a ditch to the footpath that ran along the bluff. At the edge she lay down on her stomach and looked over.

The smell of rotting seaweed and lank vegetation rose from behind the tide wall. A tangle of spindly trees and bushes cascaded down the bluff's edge, hiding what lay beneath. In one spot, the thin stalks shuddered wildly.

"*Aaaaugh!*"

What a shame, Fiona thought. Someone down there must've slipped into the muck.

Again silence. The leaves shook, then..."*Oof!*"

Fiona watched as the shivering leaves showed Lisa's progress through the narrow space between bluff and rotting wood. Finally, her cousin emerged from behind the wall. Black, oily mud coated her sneakers and most of her left leg.

Fiona melted back and crouched behind a thick bush. Gravel and shale skidded down the bluff. Lisa had made it to the second clue on the map.

A few minutes later, Lisa's head topped the bluff. She heaved herself up and rubbed the back of her hand against her forehead, leaving a dusty smear. Blood trickled from a scrape on one knee, but she didn't seem to notice. Pulling the map from her pocket, she studied it for a moment then trotted toward the road.

Lisa's perfect look was getting ragged. Fiona bit her lip, a little surprised her cousin hadn't given up right away. But Lisa would quit for sure when she realized the "blasted tree" stood in the middle of a snake and spitbug field.

Keeping low, Fiona stalked her cousin. Lisa jumped the ditch, crossed the road, and plunged into the high weeds. She didn't stop until she reached the tree – and then it was only to consult the map.

From the road, Fiona circled the trail and waited. Lisa would turn back any second now.

The giant spiders came next.

"*Oh...gross!*" Lisa's cry shot across the road.

Fiona smiled in triumph. That was it. She'd won. Now all she had to do was tell Lisa about the payback trick – and gloat all summer.

The salmonberry bushes rustled. Fiona ducked behind a shrub. A moment later, Lisa broke out from the bushes, swiping at her clothes and stamping her feet. Her hair blew in sticky clumps.

"I don't believe it," Fiona whispered.

How could perfect, snobby Lisa keep going? Why would she keep going? The Vickers were rich – she couldn't need pirate treasure.

Once again, Lisa took out the map, and with deep breaths, consulted it. Eyes narrowed, she gazed toward the shore near town. Then she headed toward the public dock.

Slowly, Fiona followed. By the time she reached the beach, her cousin had scaled the mound of tires, driftwood and debris that blocked the beach, and was jogging toward the pier.

Fiona stopped by the rubbish heap. A hundred feet away, the sun shone on the massive dock. People walked back and forth between moored boats. A man and boy fished off the end. The surrounding water was crowded with the boats of patient fishermen.

But underneath, the water had a black, oily look. Waves slapped tar-coated pylons. Even the sand smelled rotten.

Lisa ducked into the shadows and disappeared from view.

"Lisa, wait!" The wind carried away Fiona's shout. She shifted from one foot to another, unsure what to do.

A shriek ripped through the air.

Fiona scrambled over the rubbish and tore toward the dock. "I'm coming, Lisa!"

She dove under the wooden beams, into the stench of rotting fish and seaweed. Where was her cousin?

"Lisa!" she cried.

"Fiona! Is that you?" Lisa yelled.

"I'm coming!" Fiona stumbled through the dank sand, banging her head on a tar-covered beam. She scanned the area and gasped.

Lisa had plunged into the water and was struggling out against waist-high waves. The tide was coming in.

Fiona ran into the water, clenching her teeth at the shock of cold. Waves swirled around her legs. She struggled farther out until she could grab her cousin's arm.

"Are you okay?"

"Let go!" Lisa shoved back.

Fiona lost her balance and went under. She came up spluttering through a mouthful of salty water. "Aren't you drowning?"

"What? No!" Lisa pulled her up. "I found it! I found it!" she yelled.

"Found what!"

"Treasure! I found pirate treasure!"

"*What?*"

"There!" Lisa pointed. Thirty feet out, a battered metal box was tied to one of the dock's support beams. It was barely visible in the half-light.

Fiona steadied herself against the surging waves. "Lisa, that's impossible."

Her cousin dove forward into the surf.

"Lisa!"

Fiona struck out after her. The waves pushed and jostled. She grazed her side painfully against one of the pylons. Green seaweed caught in her fingers.

"It's too deep!" Fiona shouted.

Lisa kept swimming. The box gleamed dully in the half light.

Fiona took a deep breath and dove under the waves, frog-stroking toward her cousin. She twisted to miss another pylon. The dock creaked. Waves sluiced and pounded.

She gasped for air and dove under again.

Lisa made it. Fiona surfaced beside her. Together they clung to the seaweed-covered pylon, bobbing with the rise and fall of waves. Above, the dock rumbled and thumped with the tramp of people's feet.

Lisa's hair stuck to her forehead and she gasped for breath. "We've got to get it! Can you reach?"

Fiona extended her arm. Her fingers didn't even graze the bottom of the log – another foot and a half to the box.

"I'll hoist you," Lisa panted. "You're the lightest."

Fiona nodded and stepped onto her cousin's knees, then into her cupped hands.

Fiona stretched upward. Her fingers brushed the beam, then her foot slipped.

"Ow...watch it!" Lisa gasped as she surfaced.

Once again, Lisa made a ladder of her body. Using the seaweed-streaked pylon to steady herself, Fiona tried again.

She could touch the latch now; her fingers tugged at it. Suddenly, Lisa's hands gave out. Fiona splashed backwards into the water.

She came up spluttering again.

"Sorry!"

Treading water, the two girls stared up at the box.

"One more time?" Lisa asked.

"Can you manage?"

Lisa nodded. Ignoring the seaweed and splinters, she flung her arm around the pylon for support. "Ready!"

Fiona stepped from her cousin's knee up onto her shoulders. The weight pushed Lisa's face half under water, but she held on.

The box was within reach. Fiona tugged the knots that lashed it to the pier. Hemp – waterlogged and tight. Lisa surged up for air. Fiona's knee grazed wood, driving in splinters. She gasped, but kept reaching for the clasp.

"Hang on, Lisa! I've nearly got it!" she cried.

Fiona forced up the rusted lid and groped inside. Little bundles wound in tight, coarse cloth.

"I can't..." Lisa cried and collapsed.

As she tumbled into the surging water, Fiona grabbed a lump of cloth. Even while she struggled up for air, she kept her fist closed.

"It's no use!" Lisa panted when Fiona surfaced. "We have to get a boat."

Fiona nodded, too out of breath to speak. Together they rode the waves back, crawled out from under the dock and sprawled on the hot sand.

"I can't believe I found pirate treasure!" Lisa exulted.

Butterflies stomped around in Fiona's stomach. She took a deep breath. "Lisa, it's not pirate treasure – just an old tackle box. See..." Fiona opened her fist and unwound the wet cloth.

A flash of light dazzled their eyes. The sun glinted over an emerald and diamond bracelet.

Chapter 11

Now You See It...

The sunlight sparkled rainbows and green fire from the bracelet's diamonds and emeralds. Fiona dangled it from her fingers, twisting it one way, then another to catch the light.

"Treasure!" Lisa breathed.

Fiona jumped to her feet. "A boat! We've got to get a boat!"

Lisa surged up after her. They tore along the sand, sneakers squelching. When they reached the boathouse. Lisa threw open the doors.

Empty.

"Where's the boat?" Fiona shrieked.

"Marcus! He's gone fishing."

"What do we do now?"

Lisa leaned against the grey wood wall and ran her fingers through her tangled hair.

"Think!" she commanded herself.

"Can we borrow one?" Fiona asked.

"Yes! Tiffany has a boat!"

They clattered up the steps and crossed the lawn toward the main house. With an astounding leap, Lisa jumped the railing.

"Lisa!" Aunt Irene's mouth hung open in surprise. The person on the other end of the phone kept right on talking.

"Are you all right?" her mother demanded. "Did you have an accident?"

"No, Mom! Everything's fine."

Aunt Irene frowned, but put the phone back to her ear. "...I couldn't agree more. You'd think that boy would confess...No, I'm sure they'll find your emerald bracelet. It's so distinctive..."

Lisa stiffened. Fiona swallowed and slid her hand into her pocket. The girls' eyes met in shock.

"...Now don't forget, eight o'clock on Thursday," Aunt Irene continued. "We're looking forward to seeing you..."

Without speaking the girls went up to their bedroom, closed the door, and ignoring their wet clothes, sat on the window seat.

Fiona took the bracelet from her pocket. "It was stolen."

"How could I have been so dense?" Lisa exclaimed. "The pirates left about a hundred years before the pier was built..."

She stopped and stared at her cousin. "Fiona, how did you find me?"

Fiona looked down. She'd gone too far – way too far. The whole revenge idea was stupid, stupid, *stupid*.

She took a deep breath. "I made the treasure map and planted it in that book – payback for being so rotten to me."

"A trick!"

"Which you fell for!"

"I can't believe you!" Lisa jumped up. "I knew it would be like this when you came."

"What's the matter, Lisa?" retorted Fiona. "Can't you take a joke? Like when you made me feel like I was part of the gang, and then dumped me on the beach without even a flashlight!"

"Oh, shut up!" Lisa threw herself on the bed. "Now what am I going to do...?"

"Who cares?" Unable to sit still, Fiona paced the room, then stopped in front of the window. Out on the passage, she could just make out Marcus slamming the boat across the waves.

In the far regions of the house, the phone rang. A moment later there was a knock on the door.

"Telephone for you, Fiona," Mrs. Glee told her. "On the house line."

Giving Lisa a furious look on her way out, Fiona went downstairs to the kitchen.

"Hello?"

"Hi, sweetie," a thin, tired voice answered.

"Mom!" Fiona squealed. "Mom, how are you?"

"I'm good, baby. A little shaky. How about you? Are you okay?"

Fiona didn't even hesitate. "Yeah, I'm great."

"Oh, good. I had a bad dream about you. It scared me so I decided to call...Are you getting along with Lisa okay?"

"Yeah. We've been out on the beach all morning."

"That's good.... Want to talk to Dad?"

Before Fiona could answer, her dad's voice came on the line. "Hi, Fiona. I told Mom you're okay, but you know how she is – wouldn't settle down until she called."

"Everything's fine," Fiona answered.

"Good. I'm going to hang up and let your mom rest. She's doing really well, but she needs lots of sleep right now."

"I understand. Bye."

"Bye, Funny-face." The phone clicked.

Fiona put down the receiver and angrily wiped her eyes. She looked up in surprise as Mrs. Glee handed her a tissue. "Your mom all right?"

Fiona blew her nose. "I've just been worrying a lot."

Mrs. Glee nodded. "Family worry eats away at a person. Makes you a little crazy sometimes. Well, I got work to do. Mrs. Vickers wants everything just right for that party. As if any of those people would notice, anyhow."

Mrs. Glee stomped away. Fiona went back upstairs. Lisa ignored her.

Fiona sat on the side of her bed, holding clenched fists over her stomach. She didn't want to fight with her cousin all summer. She especially didn't want Mom picking up angry, lonely thoughts.

Fiona took a deep breath. "Lisa, how about a truce? The map was a payback for the way you treated me. As far as I'm concerned, we're even."

When her cousin didn't answer, Fiona picked up the bracelet. Sunlight refracted through the jewels, shining rainbows around the room. "What are we going to do about this?"

Lisa glared. "Just how did you know where the stolen jewelry was? Who told you about it?"

"Nobody! The dock was just the slimiest place I could find."

"I guess the thief decided the same thing," Lisa said slowly.

Fiona nodded. "We'd better call the cops."

"No way!" Lisa's jumped up and snatched the bracelet. "They'll think Derek told me and that I'm just trying to get the reward."

"Reward? What reward?"

"The insurance companies are offering ten percent of the value of the stolen jewelry to whoever finds it."

"All right!" Fiona breathed.

"No, it isn't. We can't collect it."

"Lisa, we're *entitled* to the reward." Already Fiona imagined the tired look fading from her dad's face when she handed him the reward money. She could help. Really help!

"The box might prove who the thief is." Lisa stared thoughtfully at the bracelet in her hand.

"When we tell the police, they'll figure it out."

Lisa shook her head. She crossed the room to her desk, and stashed the bracelet inside an old sketchbook. "I can't risk it."

"What are you doing? That's stolen property!"

"I'm not going to keep it!" Lisa snapped. "Look, if the police get the box and there aren't any clues, they'll think this bracelet is proof against Derek. Somebody's already used his jacket to make him look guilty."

"Maybe *he* used his jacket – at the robbery! How do you know he didn't?"

"Because he told me."

Fiona eyed her cousin. "When?"

Lisa hesitated. "Sunday, while we were in town. I went to see him at the jail. It's awful there, Fiona, and Derek's scared. I promised I'd help. The bracelet and whatever else is in that box might be a real clue – but it might be used against him, too."

"It might also be the only way I can help my family." Fiona went to the window and stared at the mountains. Derek didn't look like a thief. But then what does a thief look like?

If she called the police right now, Fiona was sure she'd get the reward. But what about Derek?

Lisa was right. Nobody would believe they found the bracelet by accident. They'd think Derek stole the jewelry and told Lisa where he'd stashed it.

And what if Derek really was innocent? She didn't think getting a reward for sending the wrong person to jail would help her family at all. It would be like blood money.

"Won't you help me?" Lisa said. "Please."

Fiona turned back to her cousin. "Okay. We'll get the box and check it out for clues ourselves."

Lisa nodded. "Tonight. No one will see us then."

Chapter 12

...Now You Don't

The house was dark and silent when Fiona and Lisa crept downstairs. Without a sound, they glided past the study door, then through the kitchen. Lisa unlocked the back door and they slipped outside.

"Thank goodness the alarm's still broken," Lisa whispered. "I don't know if I could've turned it off."

The moonlight stretched the dark shadows of bushes across the lawn. Fiona shivered.

Lights were still on in the Glee's cottage. Music screamed through the open windows, nearly drowning the sound of the surf.

"Marcus! Marcus! Turn that noise down!" Mrs. Glee's voice carried louder than the music.

The volume of the music went up.

The girls ran lightly down the steps to the dock. The boathouse door was latched. Fiona struggled with the hasp, trying to get the rusty bolt to slide without noise.

"Let me." Lisa gave the latch on the door a twist, then slid the bolt back. "You have to have the knack."

Inside, it was pitch black. Fiona heard the door gently close behind her, then Lisa's footsteps to the right. A cupboard door squeaked; a heavy-duty flashlight clicked on. It's beam showed the U-shaped cut-out floor. Between the arms of the U, the boat bobbed in black water.

"We have to get the outer doors open." Lisa circled around to the far side and took hold of one of the big doors. Fiona took the other.

Creak!

Fiona held her breath. Marcus' music must've drowned the sound. Lisa was already untying the boat.

"We'll row it," she whispered. "Even over the music, they'd hear the motor."

Fiona nodded. She climbed down the rickety wet ladder to the water level. With a grunt, she clambered into the boat.

Lisa came next. She handed the flashlight to Fiona.

"Hold it still." She fitted the oars into the oarlocks, and then with careful pulls, eased the boat out into open water. Waves rippled gently. Lisa rowed steadily, parallel to the shore, toward the public dock.

"Want me to take a turn?" Fiona asked after several minutes.

"Sure. This boat was made for a motor – not for oars."

After a few erratic circles, Fiona got the hang of it and began stroking toward the dock.

Peering into the night, Fiona shivered. Except for the lights on shore and a lantern on an anchored sailboat, everything was dark. The only sounds were the distant beat of Marcus' music, the *lap, lap* of water and *creak, creak* of oars.

The girls traded places one more time.

"Am I heading in the right direction?" Lisa asked after several minutes. She twisted around to look. "Everything looks different at night."

The moon broke from the clouds, casting patterns and weird shadows on the restless water.

"*The moon was a ghostly galleon, tossed upon cloudy seas...*" quoted Fiona.

"Give me a break," Lisa replied.

"Careful," Fiona said. "We're almost at the dock."

The tide had dropped since the afternoon. The timbers stood upright like giant black skeletons, creaking eerily in the night. Fiona swallowed and peered into the shadows.

The oars dipped and splashed as Lisa steered the boat between the pylons. Abruptly the moonlight disappeared. Fiona switched on the flashlight. The beam barely penetrated the dark.

"Where's the box?" Lisa leaned forward, eyes searching the timbers.

"I can't see it."

"Keep looking. It has to be there."

Fiona stood up in the boat and slowly shone the light over the pylons, one by one. The beam stopped suddenly.

"Find it?" Lisa twisted eagerly.

Fiona played the light over the wood. Nothing – except a frayed rope hanging down toward the water.

"It's gone!"

Lisa pulled on the oars. Fiona grabbed one end of the dangling rope and examined it by the light of the flashlight.

"It's been cut through. Whoever took the box didn't bother to untie the knots." She let go and sank down on the seat of the boat.

So much for the reward. So much for her chance to help her family.

"Now what?" Lisa said.

"Let's look around, just in case."

Slowly, Lisa rowed back and forth under the dock while Fiona shone the flashlight into every little crack of the wet timbers. Nothing.

Finally, Lisa turned the boat and pulled out from under the dock.

"Here, you row for a while," she said. "My arms are sore."

They traded places. Fiona began rowing back along the beach. Lisa leaned over the side, hand slapping the crests of small waves. "Who do you suppose took it?"

Fiona stopped, letting the boat drift. "I don't know. Maybe someone saw us."

"Who? Nobody would pay attention." Lisa looked up. "Unless he'd hidden his loot under there…"

"…And was keeping an eye on it." Fiona finished. "Is Derek still in jail?"

"I told you he's innocent."

"Everybody else has told me he's guilty and I need the reward. So, is Derek still in jail?"

Lisa's eyes glittered. "Yes. No thanks to my dad." She clenched her fists. "I asked him for money to pay Derek's bail and hire a lawyer. He said no and ordered me to stay away from Derek."

"Can you blame him?" Fiona demanded. "If your dad thinks Derek's guilty, he's not going to give him money."

"He should have listened to me!"

"Why? You never talk to anyone unless you want something," Fiona snapped.

For several minutes they sat silently.

"You never believed Derek is innocent either, did you?" Lisa asked.

"I could've called the police and told them about the box," Fiona told her.

"So why didn't you?"

Fiona shrugged. "Just because I drew a treasure map doesn't mean I turned into a pirate. I'm not going to make someone look guilty because I need money!"

Lisa nodded. "Truce?"

"Truce." Fiona started rowing again.

A moment later, Lisa began to giggle. "I can't believe I fell for that dumb map...and thought I'd found buried treasure!"

"Buried! You didn't even dig!"

"I have an independent mind." The boat rocked as the girls laughed. "And we found a treasure anyway!" Lisa gasped.

Fiona sagged back, taking deep breaths. "Treasure..." she repeated. Her mind raced. "Lisa, the box going missing is proof that Derek's innocent."

"So what? No one but us knew it was there."

"Us and the thief," Fiona said. "If we find the box, we find the thief."

"Except that there are about a million places to hide things around here," Lisa said. "I don't think another fake map will help."

Fiona grinned. "Do you want to row for awhile?"

The girls changed places. Fiona peered into the shadows, trying to spot which lights belonged to Vickers Villa. "Good thing that only your mom's ring was stolen. Doesn't she have a bunch of jewelry in her bedroom?"

Lisa nodded and pulled on the oars. "In the safe there. Do you think the thief would have gone for that, too, if you hadn't interrupted him?"

Fiona swallowed. "No way. I mean he wouldn't, not with your parents sleeping right there."

"He did at Tiffany's house," Lisa argued. "Her family wasn't supposed to be home that night," she admitted.

On shore, a car engine roared. Both girls jumped. The boat shimmied in the water.

"What if he comes back?" Lisa asked finally.

Butterflies flapped faster and faster in Fiona's stomach. "He can't. I mean, why would he? There are lots of easier places to rob."

"The alarm's broken and Dad can't get it replaced until next week," Lisa argued. "The burglar's already checked out our house! He must know there is even more to steal!"

"It'll be okay," Fiona insisted. "Whoever set Derek up won't dare commit any more robberies.

The police will know Derek's innocent because he's still in jail."

"Until tomorrow afternoon. His uncle is sending bail money." Lisa yanked on the oars. The boat lurched forward. "My house is on the hit list and Derek will be blamed."

"But the missing box proves he's innocent," Fiona reminded her.

"Missing means it's gone!" retorted Lisa. "We don't have anything we can show anybody."

Fiona stared across the water, thinking hard. "We will if we catch the thief."

"Right. How are we supposed to do that?" Lisa slapped the oars into the water.

"I don't know. But we'll think of something. We've got to."

"Your turn," Lisa grunted. Once again they swapped places. Fiona lifted the oars and began to row across the dark water. Her arms ached. She wished they could turn on the motor.

"Watch out – we're almost at the boathouse."

The boathouse's wide doors hung open. Fiona concentrated on steering the boat through the black square between them.

"Oof, sorry," Fiona grunted as the prow banged into the side of the dock.

"Here, let me help," a gruff voice shot through the dark. The boathouse light switched on. Horrified, Fiona and Lisa looked up to see Marcus smiling down at them.

Fiona slowly let her breath out. "What are you doing here?"

Marcus crouched down to grab the mooring rope and tied the prow of the boat before answering. "Just getting my lures and bait ready for tomorrow. I'm going fishing early." He held out his hand to help Lisa up from the boat. "What were you two up to? Looking for more treasure?"

"How did you know about that?" Fiona demanded.

Marcus laughed. "Oh, I was fishing near the dock this afternoon. You were yelling so loud that half the island must've heard. What happened? Did you find some money in the sand or something?"

"No." Fiona and Lisa exchanged looks. "Did you see anyone else?"

"Didn't notice anybody, but I didn't look either." He smiled. "I hooked this twelve pound salmon. Did he give me a fight! But I landed him. Salmon steaks for a week! And I'm going for his big brother, first thing tomorrow."

He went to the work table against the wall and started sorting through the lures and floats spread out there. The girls watched silently.

"We think we found the jewelry stolen during the break-ins," Lisa told him abruptly.

Marcus looked around. "You found what?"

"Except now it's gone," Fiona added.

Marcus stared at them. "Didn't the cops get the jewelry when they arrested Derek?"

"Derek didn't rob anybody, so he didn't have the jewelry." Lisa's voice held an icy edge.

"Seems hard to believe he did it," Marcus agreed. "We didn't hang out together, but I always figured Derek for an okay guy." He reached down for the tackle box under the table.

Fiona's eyes followed his movements. She gasped. The box Marcus lifted up was rusted and battered like the one hidden under the dock.

"That's it! That's the box! Marcus, you snake, you took the treasure!"

Chapter 13

Prowlers in the Night

Fiona darted across the boathouse and wrenched the tackle box from Marcus' hands. Putting it on the floor, she snapped the clasps and pulled open the rust-streaked lid – revealing trays of lures and tackle.

"Well, I got some good lures, but I wouldn't exactly call them treasure." Marcus picked up his box and put it back on the work table.

Fiona stared at him, unbelieving.

"I'm going to bed." Lisa turned and headed for the door.

Face burning, Fiona followed her cousin outside, up the steps, and across the grass.

"Hi, girls!"

Fiona squealed. A shadow stepped out from a tall clump of bushes.

"Bruce!" Lisa hissed. "What are you doing here?"

The gardener held up an electric hedge clipper. "Forgot my trimmer."

"Well, you've got it now," Lisa said. She tried to walk past him, but he stood in their way.

"It isn't real safe for kids your age to be out this late." His voice sounded menacing.

"Why should you care what we do?" Lisa demanded.

"Mr. Vickers might not be pleased to hear you've been sneaking out at night."

Fiona's chin went up. "He might not be pleased to know what Sergeant Reese said to you, either."

Bruce seemed amused. "Are you threatening me?"

Fiona shrugged. "You're in our way. Good night!"

She walked around the gardener. Lisa followed. At the kitchen door, the girls stopped and checked behind them. Bruce had disappeared.

"What about Sergeant Reese and Bruce?" Lisa demanded.

Fiona told her about the conversation she'd overheard. "And then Reese tried to order Bruce off the island."

Lisa shivered. "The guy's really weird. And our alarm's still broken. Do you think he's planning something?"

"I don't know," Fiona said. "Maybe he's really the thief."

Lisa shook her head. "He showed up after the robberies started."

"I'm sure he's connected," Fiona argued. "I feel it in my gut."

Lisa giggled. "That's hunger."

Fiona grinned. "Maybe. Or maybe Bruce saw something, too." She paused. "You know, Marcus' box sure looked like the same one."

"Tackle boxes all look the same and Marcus has had that one for ages." Lisa yawned. "I'm going to bed. Coming?" Without looking back, she went into the house.

"I guess." Fiona started to follow, then stopped again. She had to get one more look at that box.

"Lisa!" she whispered. But her cousin had already disappeared.

Fiona hesitated only a second. Keeping an eye out for Bruce, she ran across the lawn and down to the boathouse. She crouched under a window and slowly lifted her head. The glass was so smeared with cobwebs and grime, that to see through it, she had to wipe it with the bottom of her shirt.

Marcus was still messing around with his lures and bait, and singing to music blasting from his phone.

She watched for nearly half an hour. Finally Marcus packed his gear away, put the tackle box next to the boat, and then switched out the light.

Fiona pressed against the wall as Marcus came out. Without glancing in her direction, he climbed the stairs to the cottage. The phone bobbed in his hand. Music throbbed along with him.

Breathing hard, Fiona pushed open the door of the boathouse and went in. By touch, she retrieved the flashlight and began searching.

Cans of paint, glue, and boat varnish lined a few shelves. A rusty assortment of hammers, saws and tools hung from a peg board. Life jackets, spare oars, and a couple of old bicycles hung on the opposite wall.

That was it.

Not ready to give up, Fiona crouched down by Marcus' tackle box.

Trying to remember, she shut her eyes and imagined she was still in the water with Lisa holding her up. She felt over the snaps, pictured forcing up the lid and groping inside. Her fingers followed her remembered movements. Was it the right box?

She wasn't sure. Frustrated, Fiona shut the lid.

She heard a sound outside! Fiona froze, breathing hard. Was Marcus coming back? Snapping off the flashlight, she looked around for somewhere to hide. The room was bare – no where to take cover...except....

Dropping the flashlight, Fiona climbed onto the rickety ladder.

Black water swirled nearly to the third rung. With a gasp, Fiona plunged down. Cold washed over her knees...hips...stomach...to her shoulders.

The boathouse door squealed open. Fiona sank lower then swung around the ladder under the boathouse floor.

A flashlight shone around the bare walls. Footsteps crossed and recrossed the wooden floor above her head. Something swimming brushed Fiona's leg. She gasped, then bit her lip to keep from crying out.

Marcus would've turned on the light. Whoever this was, he didn't want to be seen... and he was searching the boathouse.

Fiona craned her neck to catch a glimpse of the intruder. No luck. Was it Bruce? Or the thief?

What if the burglar had been watching? Waiting for whoever took the emerald bracelet to come back for the rest of the jewels....

Fiona sank farther down in the water. She didn't care what was swimming below.

Finally, the flashlight switched off and the boathouse door squealed again. Shivering,

Fiona climbed out of the water. She stumbled to the door and peered out.

The coast was clear.

Clothes plastered to her body, she scurried up the steps toward the house. Music still pounded from the Glee's cottage. Mrs. Glee still ragged on and on at Marcus. The music went up a notch louder.

It hadn't been Marcus in the boathouse. Fiona tried to wring out a corner of her shirt, then giving up, went in the kitchen door.

Still shivering, she locked the door then made her way through the downstairs rooms. Nervously glancing behind her, Fiona groaned. She'd left a trail. Water puddled everywhere.

Grimly, she returned to the kitchen, got out the mop, and swished it back and forth over her tracks. When she put the mop back in the cupboard, a dustpan fell, clattering loudly across the floor. Fiona froze.

Nothing. She let out her breath.

Creak!

Footsteps. On the main staircase! The thief had broken in!

"Aunt Irene! Uncle Harold!" Fiona shouted. "Call the cops! *Quick!*"

The lights flipped on. Uncle Harold stared owlishly from the hall. Behind, Aunt

Irene clutched his shoulder. Lisa slid past his arm. Scott, armed with his water rifle, followed.

"*Fiona?*" Lisa demanded. "What happened to you?"

"Where's the robber?" Scott brandished his weapon. "I'll get him!"

Pounding started at the kitchen door. Fiona shrank back, but Scott slid back the bolts. The door flew open and Marcus shot in. "I saw lights in here, then I heard someone yelling. Everything okay?"

"Fiona was getting another midnight snack," Lisa giggled.

"Thanks a lot," Fiona hissed.

Aunt Irene stared at her. "Fiona, dear... you're all wet."

"I...uh...decided to go swimming..."

"In your clothes?" Uncle Harold asked.

Fiona looked helplessly at Lisa. Her cousin tried not to laugh. "Um...yes...but then I remembered the no swimming by yourself rule and...I uh...got out...."

Aunt Irene frowned. "I'm sure that isn't quite what has happened, but I'm too tired to care."

Meanwhile, Scott scouted the perimeter. He nailed a moth fluttering around the pantry, shot the heads off a wilting bouquet of roses, and finally sent a stream of water across his mother's robe.

"Scott! Stop it!" Aunt Irene cried. "Harold! Do something."

"I'm going to bed." Her husband stalked out of the kitchen.

Lisa kept giggling.

Grinning widely, Marcus headed for the kitchen door. "Think I'll be going, Mrs. Vickers. Night, Fiona." He saluted and left, shutting the door behind him – just in time to avoid a stream of water.

"Rats," Scott declared. "I missed."

"Lisa!" Fiona demanded. "What happened?"

"I thought you were a burglar!"

"Me?" Fiona started to laugh.

"I don't know what's gotten into you two!" Aunt Irene started toward the stairs. "Scott! Come to bed."

"*Mom!*"

"Now, Scott."

With a last shot of water splattered across the floor, he followed his mom up the stairs.

"I heard someone walking around down here," Lisa explained. "So I woke up Dad."

"But you must've known it was me – I wasn't in bed!" Fiona argued.

Lisa shook her head and reached for a paper towel. "I thought you were right behind me, but you weren't. I waited and waited and then I heard the door open and someone walking around downstairs."

She handed a wad of paper towels to Fiona and together they wiped up the remains of Scott's gun-battle. "I thought the burglar had broken in and had caught you. What else was I supposed to do?"

"But it wasn't the burglar," Fiona insisted.

Lisa tossed the towels in the garbage. "Not this time."

Chapter 14

The Wrong Box

The next morning, both girls slept through breakfast. Waking up slowly, Fiona yawned and glanced across the room. Her cousin was curled up in a lump of blankets and quilts.

Lazily, Fiona gazed at the sunbeams scattered across the wall. With effort, she made herself concentrate on the missing jewelry.

Maybe someone else had gone under the dock and accidentally found the box.... No, the chances of that happening were awfully small.

Her eyes drifted to the dust motes floating on the sunbeams.... Probably the robber had just come back for it.... She yawned.... And then he'd searched the boathouse....

Fiona's suddenly came wide-awake. Somebody had hunted through the *Vickers'* *boathouse*! The robber had checked his stash and realized the bracelet was missing. He must know Fiona and Lisa had it.

The house would be next!

Shivering, Fiona pulled the quilt up around her neck. She and Lisa were in trouble. Big trouble. Her stomach knotted up. What if Mom caught her feelings of fear again? Fiona squeezed her eyes shut.

Orcas. Think about orcas....

It didn't work.

Abruptly, Fiona threw back the covers and got dressed. The only way they'd be safe would be to catch the thief. Giving the bracelet to the police wouldn't help. Even if the police believed their completely weird story about how they found it, the thief might think Fiona and Lisa knew something that could send him to jail.

Marcus could have remembered something by now – something he just hadn't paid attention to in the excitement of catching that salmon.

Fiona raced downstairs. No one answered the door at the Glee's cottage. She went down to the boathouse. Empty. The tackle box was gone and so was the boat.

Frustrated, Fiona climbed slowly back up to the house. Uncle Harold was sitting at the patio table, sipping coffee and reading on his tablet.

"Good morning," Fiona sat down in the chair beside him.

He lowered the device and took another sip of coffee, all the while regarding her. "Until you came, Fiona, this house was much quieter."

Fiona's face heated up. "Sorry, Uncle Harold. I don't try to do anything."

"Don't you really?" He turned his eyes to the tablet again. Fiona wished she could sink into the patio bricks. Instead she reached for a glass of orange juice.

"I've always thought it was a little too quiet," Uncle Harold said.

Fiona choked.

Back upstairs, Fiona slipped into the bathroom for a long, soaky, thinktank bubble-bath. When she came out, Lisa's bed was empty. From the window, she could see Lisa sitting on the driftwood log. Pixie lay at her feet.

Fiona shoved her fists into her pockets. If they'd gone back for the box right away and not waited until night, they might have solved the crime. And she would have the reward money to give to her Dad.

She had to do something!

She pulled her hair into a damp pony tail and headed down to the dock. Lisa met her there. Pixie sat patiently on the sand, watching them and scratching a few fleas.

"Now what?" Lisa said.

"We make a plan."

Hearing the purr of a motor, Fiona looked across the water. Marcus was coming back.

"Catch anything?" Fiona called as he maneuvered the boat toward the dock.

"Naw. I'll try again later though." He cut the motor and jumped onto the dock.

"Marcus," Fiona said. "Have you remembered anything else about yesterday afternoon? Did you see anyone hanging around the dock?"

"Sorry, kid." He tied the mooring rope. "But I've been thinking. You'd better not tell anyone else you found that jewelry."

"Why not?" Fiona asked.

"It's not going to do Derek any good, anyway," added Lisa.

"Forget Derek for a minute. If the cops think you knew where the jewelry was and didn't say anything, they might charge you as an accessory."

"A what?" Fiona demanded.

"An accessory. You know, somebody that helps the thief out or hides evidence. Like on the TV shows."

"They couldn't do that...could they?" Fiona bit her lip. More trouble. And the bracelet hidden in Lisa's sketchbook would really nail them.

Marcus shrugged, hauled his tackle box out of the boat and put it on the dock. "Why take a chance? And if the stuff's gone, what good would talking do anyway?"

"It's the only clue we had that proved Derek's innocent," Lisa insisted.

"But you haven't got it any more," Marcus pointed out.

Fiona stared down at the tackle box, trying to see some detail that would prove it was the missing one. "That really looks like the box that was under the dock."

"Give it a rest, Fiona," Marcus said. "If I'd found the jewelry, I'd cash it in for the reward and be long gone." He crouched down. "This box belonged to my father. See, his initials are right here."

He flipped open the lid. Screwed to the underside was a tarnished metal plate engraved with the letters, *MBG*. "Marcus Benjamin Glee, my father."

Marcus shut the lid again. "My Dad gave me this before he left. So keep your hands off it." He carried it into the boathouse.

"He's sure touchy."

"His dad walked out on them three years ago – that's when Mrs. Glee started working here," Lisa said. "And he's right, Fiona. Tackle boxes all look the same."

"But where *is* the box?" Fiona insisted. "Everything depends on finding the stolen jewelry."

"I know that. I just don't know how to do it!"

"We're not getting anywhere," Fiona said. "Let's get something to eat. I think better on a full stomach."

Lisa nodded and together they climbed the steps to the house. Aunt Irene was at the patio table, phone to her ear.

"No, no, Rachel...I quite understand. We do seem to be having a lot of family excitement this summer..." Her laugh sounded forced.

Lisa and Fiona exchanged a look of bewilderment.

"Yes...Of course Scott will be thrilled to have a week with both his cousins...."

"What?" Fiona and Lisa gasped in unison. Aunt Irene shot them an exasperated look.

"...yes...yes, dear," Aunt Irene said into the phone. "No, just pack a bag for each of them and drop them at Harold's office in Seattle. They can ride here with him... yes...no...don't work too hard, now.... Bye." She flicked the off switch and turned her bewildered gaze to the girls.

"Your Aunt Rachel's been offered a wonderful promotion," she said. "But it means she has to leave for a manager's meeting in Portland tomorrow. I...um...said I'd look after the boys while she's gone."

"Jimmy?" Fiona demanded.

"*And* Ryan?" Lisa groaned.

"Yes..." Aunt Irene blinked. "Oh dear, I hope Mrs. Glee...and my party...I suppose I'd better call Harold." She stared at the phone in dismay.

Fiona grinned. "This is great!"

"It is?" Lisa didn't look any more pleased than her mother.

"Yes," Fiona said. "Trust me."

"Perhaps you girls could help supervise the boys?" Aunt Irene asked hopefully. "I could pay you?"

"*Mom!* I don't have time to baby-sit my cousins," Lisa said.

Fiona gave her a look. "Ryan is eleven and Jimmy is ten," she said. "Probably they won't need to be baby-sat, Aunt Irene. In fact, if you tell them what you want done, they could help out. I know Ryan does housework all the time, and Jimmy vacuums our place."

"They do?" Aunt Irene looked astonished.

"Absolutely," confirmed Fiona. "And if you'll tell me where you want them to sleep, Lisa and I will make up the beds."

Aunt Irene began to look much less harassed. "Well...if you don't mind...and then Mrs. Glee could concentrate on my party...."

A few minutes later, Lisa pulled sheets and pillowcases from the linen closet and piled them into Fiona's arms. "I don't see why you're so pleased Jimmy and Ryan are coming," she grumbled.

"Because if we're going to trap the thief, we need all the reinforcements we can get," Fiona told her.

"I wouldn't exactly call them reinforcements."

Fiona headed toward the guest room beside Scott's bedroom. "That's because you try and do everything yourself."

Lisa threw back the bedspread on the closest twin bed and snapped open one of the sheets. "They're just kids. They'll mess things up."

"And we didn't?" Fiona grabbed her side and pulled it straight.

Lisa grinned and tucked in the corner. "What about that plan?"

Fiona slid the pillow into the pillowcase and plopped it on the bed. "I'm thinking."

By the time the second bed was made, Scott had heard the news of his cousins coming. He leaned against the door jamb, water rifle at the ready.

"One step into my room and wham!" he shot a stream of water at the girls.

"Scott!" Lisa shrieked.

Fiona ducked. The water splatted against the window. "If your mom sees you do that," she warned, "you'll be dead meat."

Scott shrugged. "I don't care!"

"Look, we made a deal that I'd tell Jimmy to lay off. Besides," she glanced at Lisa, who frowned then nodded, "we're going to need your help. And Jimmy's and Ryan's too."

"With what?" Scott lowered the rifle.

Fiona told him about finding and losing the jewelry, how it proved Derek was innocent, and their worry about the thief coming back to rob Vickers Villa. Scott's grip on the water gun tightened.

"We don't have proof of anything, so nobody's going to believe us," she said. "We've got to trap the thief."

"How?" Scott demanded.

"We're working on it."

Scott took aim at the window again. "I'll nail him."

"Yeah, right," Lisa snapped. "A shot of water will stop him dead."

Scott swung the nose of the plastic rifle toward her. She dove behind the bed just in time.

"Hit the floor, Lisa!" he taunted.

"Scott, knock it off," Fiona told him. "Are you in or not?"

Scott nodded. "I'm in." As Lisa sprang from behind the bed, he dashed out of the bedroom. "But I'm going for some target practice," he called back.

Lisa raced after him, then gave up and came back. "We'll use my brother as bait," she said. "I'm willing to make the sacrifice."

Chapter 15

To Catch a Thief

When Fiona and Lisa left the house, Bruce the gardener was slowly trimming the shrubs by the patio.

"Getting ready for the party?" Fiona asked.

"Following orders," the man said glumly. The clipper sputtered. With a growl of frustration, the man shook the machine.

"The cord is unplugged," Fiona pointed out. Bruce was the worst gardener ever. Judging from the scratches on his arms and the half-cut blackberries at the foot of the lawn, he didn't even know how to cut back the aggressive canes.

"Have you been a gardener for long?" she asked, eyeing his uneven hedge trim.

"Too long." He scowled, pushed the plug back in, and pressed the trigger on the trimmer.

"Fiona, come on!" Lisa called from the dock.

Reluctantly, Fiona crossed the lawn and joined her. Derek was waiting, too, half in the shadows.

"What were you doing?" Lisa demanded when she reached them.

Fiona shrugged. "Trying to be friendly to Bruce...in case he's noticed anything."

"The police already questioned him," Lisa said dismissively, then she leaned toward Derek. "Are you sure you're okay?"

"I'm fine." Derek told her.

Fiona didn't think he looked fine. His face was white and there were dark rings under his eyes. Lisa looked him over searchingly.

"We're going to prove you're innocent," she said.

Derek slumped against the boathouse wall. "That would be a good trick."

"We've already got some clues." Lisa told him about finding and losing the stolen jewelry.

"If we trap the thief, we can convince the police," Fiona added.

"Don't even try," Derek said. "You might get hurt. Besides, the court lawyer says if I plead guilty, they'll probably give me a suspended sentence because I'm only fifteen and all the jails are full anyway."

"But you aren't guilty!" Lisa exclaimed.

Derek forced a smile. "Disappearing evidence won't help me. If I fight the charges and lose, I'll go to jail."

"There's a principle!" Lisa insisted. "You have to stick up for what you believe in, even if you might lose."

"Can't we just drop this?" Derek jumped up and began pacing.

"No, we can't," Fiona said. "There's nothing to stop the thief from breaking into the house for the rest of the jewelry. Or doesn't that bother you?"

Derek stopped pacing and turned around. "What do you mean?"

"You're out of jail and the thief has already looked over Lisa's house," Fiona reminded him. "There's a lot of valuable stuff just waiting."

"We'll be robbed," Lisa said tightly, "and you'll be blamed again."

Derek stood uncertainly. "I don't want you to get hurt."

"Then let's get this guy," Lisa declared.

Derek looked from one girl to the other. He started to pace the dock again. "The break-ins all happened while the people were out at parties – except for Tiffany's."

"And her family was supposed to be away for the weekend," Lisa said, "but Mrs. Mirosa got the flu."

"Whoever the guy is," Derek said, "he's taking crazy risks."

"What if we pretend Lisa's house is empty, but we'd actually be there waiting?" Fiona said.

"And then what do we do? Jump out and yell gotcha?" Lisa protested. "Besides, everybody was *in* our house when the thief stole Mom's ring." She slouched against the boathouse wall.

"How did he open the safe?" Fiona asked

"With the combination," Lisa answered glumly.

"Where did he get that?" Fiona demanded.

Lisa grimaced. "Mom always forgets the numbers so she has them written down in about ten places – her jewelry box, the wallet she lost, even on the bulletin board in the kitchen. They're gone now. I guess Dad made her take them down."

"Half the island could have the combinations," Derek muttered.

"Bruce!" Fiona narrowed her eyes. "Last Friday, I saw him sneak something off the kitchen bulletin board. It's him!"

"No, it isn't," Derek said. "There had already been five break-ins before Bruce showed up. I know, because he came around when I was working and asked who might need a gardener or a handyman. Some of my customers had already fired me, so there was a ready-made job waiting for him," Derek added bitterly.

Fiona peeled a splinter from the dock and tossed it in the water. "He seems like such a good suspect," she lamented. "And he's such a terrible gardener. No one would miss him."

Lisa shrugged. "Maybe we should just set a trap and see who we catch."

"Even if he is taking a lot of risks, the thief will want your folks out of the house," Fiona insisted. "It's one thing to open a downstairs safe. It's something else to go into your parent's room while they're asleep."

"But they're not going anywhere," Lisa said. "So either the burglar gives up, or...."

The three kids looked at each other. "This is so not good," Fiona said softly.

"And we can't even go to the police," Derek muttered. He scrubbed his hand over his face.

Behind them, the drone of Bruce's clippers again filled the air.

"Tomorrow night!" exclaimed Fiona. "Your parent's party is the perfect set-up!"

"No! You're out of your mind!" Lisa said aghast.

"Think about it!" Fiona insisted. "If we spread it around that Aunt Irene's jewels are going to the bank Friday morning, *because* of the break-ins, the burglar will know the party's his only chance."

"The place will be full of people," Derek argued. "What if he's too chicken?"

"He hasn't been so far." Fiona looked at the other two expectantly.

"It's worth a try," Lisa said slowly. "If he doesn't break in by tomorrow night, he'll think the jewelry's in the bank."

"What about tonight?" Derek asked.

"We'll keep watch," Lisa said.

Fiona nodded. "Scott's already in on the plan, and I bet once Jimmy and Ryan get here, they'll help too."

"I can keep an eye on things from out here," Derek said grimly. "If I see anyone, I'll grab him."

Lisa looked up in alarm. "You might get hurt."

"And if the police see you, they'll think you're hanging around to rob the place," Fiona warned.

Derek scowled and clenched his fists. "It would be worth it if I could get my hands on whoever framed me." He stared out at the water for a moment, and then turned back to the girls. "But if we tell everyone the jewelry's gone now, you won't have to risk anything," Derek said. "You'll be safe."

Lisa shook her head. "We have to catch the real thief to prove you're innocent."

Derek took a deep breath. "I'm willing to try just about anything – but not if it'll get you two in trouble...or hurt."

"I want the reward money," Fiona said.

"I want my grandmother's ring back," Lisa added.

Derek smiled. "All right, then. Let's do it! I'll go to all the places where guys I know hang out and shoot my mouth off, like I'm mad at everyone."

"We'll do the town," Lisa said.

"Meet back at the log around five?"

The girls nodded. Derek jumped down to the beach and strode away, Pixie at his heels.

At the top of the bluff, Bruce threw a clump of thorny trimmings into the pile and rubbed his scratched arms. When Fiona and Lisa reached the lawn, he called out to them. "I see Derek's out of jail."

The girls didn't answer.

"You kids spent a lot of time with your heads together. Hatching some kind of plan?"

"Nothing that's your business," Lisa snapped.

Fiona nudged her. "Actually," she said. "We were deciding whether to go into Seattle with Aunt Irene on Friday. She's putting all her jewelry in the safety deposit box after the party."

"Too bad she doesn't do it now." Bruce eyed them. "And Derek's coming along too? Seems surprising when your mom and dad think he's the local thief."

"Well, Derek isn't the thief," Lisa said coolly. "And if you'll excuse us, we have things to do."

They found Aunt Irene in the kitchen, consulting with Mrs. Glee over the menu. Fiona couldn't help but glance at the bulletin board. There was no combination posted now.

"We're going into town," Lisa said. "Anything we can do for your party, Mom?"

"Oh, yes! I just need a few more flowers... and some anchovy paste...and...I'll make you a list." She darted out of the room.

"Don't forget the artichoke hearts," Mrs. Glee called after her. "Party's ridiculous," she grumbled. "If she was in trouble, these people would lose her phone number."

"They're mom's friends," Lisa said.

"I've had that kind of friends." Mrs. Glee pulled a bunch of carrots from the fridge.

"What happened," Fiona asked.

Mrs. Glee took a peeler from the drawer. "My husband left. Then I didn't have money for rent, and my better-off friends didn't have time for me." She yanked the peeler across the carrots. Orange curls fell into the sink.

"Didn't you get child support?" Lisa asked.

"You need to find the father to get it. We lost just about everything. Marcus wanted to take off and go looking for his dad. As if we had any money to do that! But then Mrs. V offered me this job and fixed up the cottage real nice."

"I've got the list, Lisa!" Aunt Irene hurried back into the kitchen. "Can you think of anything else, Mrs. Glee?"

The housekeeper looked at the paper. "Fresh ground pepper," she said. "I'd like to see them all sneeze."

When a crowd of teenagers pushed into the ice cream shop, Lisa's and Fiona's eyes met over their milkshakes.

"Maybe Mom will take us with her to Seattle when she goes into the bank," Lisa said loudly. This was their fourth stop in town so far.

Keeping an eye out for the reaction around them, Fiona added, "We could do some shopping. Do you think she'll take long *getting into the safety deposit box*?"

Lisa shook her head. "Oh no. It only takes a minute. I'm *so* glad she's decided to take *her jewelry* to *the bank*, instead of leaving it in the house. With all these break-ins, you can't take chances."

Ginger Bocci left her friends and sauntered over to them. "Now that Derek's out on bail, the robberies are going to start again."

"Maybe," Fiona said. "The real thief might figure it's safe because everything will be blamed on Derek."

Ginger arched her eyebrows. "Excuse me, but you sound like you think that jerk is innocent."

Fiona smiled sweetly. "I like to have proof before I ruin someone's reputation."

"I know what I know," Ginger retorted.

"Which isn't much," Fiona whispered to Lisa.

Her cousin grinned and turned to Ginger. "Too bad your mom didn't put her emerald bracelet in the bank like my mom's going to. Once this party's over, no thief will be able to find anything in our house. Right, Fiona?"

Fiona took a slurp of her milkshake. "Absolutely. But I wish it were before *the party on Thursday*. I guess all the *jewelry* will be safe enough in the bedroom safe.... Safe in the safe! Get it?"

Lisa kicked her under the table.

At the thrift shop, Fiona spent some time looking at the array of used tackle boxes. Four black plastic, six red metal, and five grey metal. Three were exact duplicates of the one she'd seen under the dock. And close examination of each didn't give her a clue as to how to tell the boxes apart.

"I give up," she told Lisa.

"Told you." Her cousin nodded toward the glass jewelry cases. "Let's do our thing."

When the elderly sales woman came over, Fiona pointed to an antique silver necklace set with pale blue stones. "Is that valuable?"

The lady smiled. "Isn't it pretty? It's from old Mrs. Kreiger's estate. Only one son and he's not married so he's selling all her jewelry. A shame really."

"If you buy it, Fiona, mom will let you put it in the *bank's safety deposit box* in the city." Lisa smiled at the sales woman. "Mom is sending *all* her *jewelry* into the city right after her party on Thursday."

The lady smiled in bewilderment. "How... wise...."

Fiona decided against buying the necklace.

When Derek met the girls on the beach at the end of the afternoon, he assured them that everybody'd heard about the supposed safe keeping of the jewelry.

"I've been playing basketball and pool for hours," he reported. "And the entire time, I whined and complained about the bum rap I got and how Mrs. Vickers is locking up her jewelry because I'm friends with Lisa." He shook his head and grinned. "This better work because I made myself sound like the world's biggest loser."

Lisa grimaced. "We giggled and chattered like we had peanuts for brains. Talk about pathetic!"

"Look, there's Marcus," Fiona pointed to the boat slapping through the waves. "We'd better pass the story on to him too."

"I can't talk to anyone else." Lisa pulled her sketchpad out of her bag and flipped it open. "Tell me about it later."

Fiona and Derek slogged along the beach and sprawled on the dock as though they'd been lazing in the sun all afternoon.

The motorboat slowed. The prow bumped gently into the dock. Fiona caught the rope Marcus threw and tied it to one of the rings.

He hoisted out his tackle box and smiled. "Want to check for treasure, kid?"

"That's getting old, Marcus," Fiona said. "Besides, I've given up. Aunt Irene's gotten so worried about the break-ins, she's putting her jewelry into the safety deposit box in Seattle as soon as the party is over. There won't be anything left around here to steal."

Marcus climbed out of the boat. "Oh yeah? That'll take the heat off you, Derek."

"Looking forward to it."

Carrying his tackle box, Marcus headed up toward the cottage.

"Why does everybody fish around here?" Fiona asked. "He goes out a couple of times a day but hardly catches anything."

Derek grinned. "It's great to be out on the water, just sitting and daydreaming. Fishing's an excuse to get there."

They went back to the log and sprawled comfortably in the sand.

"Now that we've got the rumors spread," Lisa said. "How are we going to catch the robber?"

Fiona bit her lip. "I've been thinking about the kind of clues police look for. We need the thief to leave fingerprints."

"So far he's been too smart," Derek pointed out.

"I know. But I remembered how when I was six, I spilled red paint into the carpet while I was making valentines."

"Thank you for sharing that," retorted Lisa.

Fiona smiled. "Nobody knew until Jimmy left little red footprints all over the house."

Lisa sat up. "How could they not know? Red paint is not easy to miss."

"Except in a red carpet," Derek supplied. "Is that right?"

Fiona nodded. "Yup. If the thief walks through paint the same color as your parent's bedroom carpet, he won't know until there are footprints all down the stairs. It's kind of like dusting for fingerprints before the person makes them."

"Fiona, you're crazy! We can't pour paint into my parent's white carpet – even white paint!"

"I know. But it's the best idea I've been able to come up with."

Gloomily, she stared out at the Sound. Lisa rubbed her hands through the sand and looked at her palms. White and brown flecks stuck to them.

"Chalk," she said abruptly.

"What?"

"Drawing chalk. Ground into powder. It would leave footprints just like paint, except we can vacuum it up afterwards and nothing would be wrecked."

"And we can put some in the safe and your mom's jewelry box too," Fiona exclaimed. "That way the thief would have it all over himself."

"He could wash it off before the cops came," Derek objected.

"Fluorescent paint powder!" Lisa said. "It doesn't look like anything until it gets wet. But when it does...he'll glow in the dark!"

"It might not rain," Derek argued.

Fiona grinned. "Who needs rain? Scott's been nailing everything that moves with his water gun."

Chapter 16

Plan B

Lisa and Fiona found Mrs. Vickers in the living room, pulling back the sheers. The afternoon light danced through the room, over the perfectly prepared room.

"Do you think the boys will want to be introduced at my party?" Lisa's mom asked. The pucker between her eyebrows showed her anxiety. "Family is so important...with your mom sick, Fiona, I see that...but it's the first party I've had this year..."

"And some of your 'friends' like Mrs. Bocci are evil," Lisa said flatly.

"Yes...well...but family's most important..." her mom's voice quavered in uncertainty. "Your father and the boys should be here soon."

"They probably won't come to the party, Aunt Irene," Fiona said. "Lisa and I've thought of a way to keep them entertained."

"You have?" Aunt Irene brightened noticeably. "Oh, my...they're here."

Uncle Harold's car came to a stop as Aunt Irene and the girls went out to meet them. The boys piled out of the back seat. Uncle Harold popped the trunk.

"Hi, Fiona!" Jimmy yelled. "How's it going?"

"Great," Fiona said.

"For real? Ryan and me are ready, y'know." He ran a suspicious glance over Lisa. "In case you need payback."

"It's all good. I've got a lot to tell you," Fiona said. "Hi, Ryan."

"Yo!" Ryan called from behind the car. He reappeared, brandishing a single-barreled fluorescent orange water rifle.

"Not you, too!" Lisa said.

"Where's our little cousin, Scottie?" he demanded.

"Up here, dog-breath!" A stream of water shot from the roof, where Scott lay commando-style, water gun pointed at his cousins. He pumped rapidly. Another burst of water sprayed down.

"Scott!" Lisa shrieked and dodged behind the car. Fiona crouched by the tire, laughing.

"Scott?" Aunt Irene called. "Scott, dear...I don't think...Harold!"

"Ambush!" Jimmy dove toward the trunk to get his own water rifle.

"Where's a hose?" Ryan demanded.

"Forget it!" Lisa wrenched the gun from his grasp.

"Scott!" Uncle Harold shouted. "Get down from there, *now*!"

Reluctantly, Scott lowered his rifle and scuttled back across the low-pitched roof to his bedroom window.

Aunt Irene looked up at the window and back at her nephews. "Oh dear," she said.

Lisa fixed Ryan with an icy glare and handed back his rifle. "We're going to talk, Ryan."

"Any time – baby." He grinned.

"Do you want to live?" Lisa asked sweetly.

The boys high-fived, slung their water guns over their shoulders, and dug their belongings out of the car trunk. To one side, Uncle Harold and Aunt Irene had a low-voiced conference.

"At least the troops are armed and ready," Fiona commented. Lisa rolled her eyes.

"Boys," Uncle Harold said.

"Yes, sir?" Jimmy answered.

"You will not shoot those water guns in the house."

"No, sir," Ryan agreed.

"And...." He fixed them with a stern look. "You will not bother your aunt, interfere with the preparations for her party, or disrupt the household."

The boys looked at each other and nodded.

"Okay..." Ryan answered.

"Sorry, Uncle Harold," Jimmy offered.

"Good. Now let's get you inside."

The kids picked up the duffel bags, knapsacks and sleeping bags and headed into the house. Uncle Harold went into his study and shut the door.

"Where should we take our stuff, Aunt Irene?" Jimmy asked.

"Oh...upstairs, dear. Scott! *Scott!* Come help your cousins! I have to discuss some arrangements with Mrs. Glee...my party, you know...*Scott!*" She hurried off in the direction of the kitchen.

Scott came slowly down the stairs, water gun gripped loosely in his hand. The boys looked each other over.

"Cool ambush," Ryan said.

"Yeah, real cool," Lisa snapped. "Spray me again, Scott, and you're dead." She turned the glare on her cousins. "That also goes for you two."

The boys exchanged long-suffering looks. Then Ryan unslung his gun and held it up. "I've got a 470. What's yours?"

Scott lifted his water gun. "A 580."

Jimmy displayed his. "Mine's a 520. It shoots about fifty feet."

Scott moved more quickly down the stairs. "Mine'll go seventy-five, easy. Dump your stuff. We can spray the sea gulls."

"All right!" Grabbing the bags, the three boys raced upstairs.

"That'll scare any thief," Lisa said. "When should we fill them in?"

Fiona glanced toward the dining room, where Aunt Irene and Mrs. Glee were arguing over which serving dishes to use.

"Tonight," she said. "We don't want anyone hearing us."

By the time a late, thrown-together dinner was served, Fiona and Lisa had planned the trap.

Fiona caught Jimmy in the hall going into the dining room. "Eight o'clock, Lisa's bedroom," she whispered. "All of you."

Jimmy gave her a bewildered look, but nodded.

At eight, armed to the teeth with yellow, orange and green water guns, the boys sauntered into the girls' bedroom.

"So, what's the scoop?" Ryan demanded.

Fiona and Lisa filled them in on the robberies, and the jewels that had been found and lost again.

"The trap's set for the party tomorrow night," Fiona finished. "Are you guys in?"

The boys exchanged looks. Jimmy pumped his water gun.

"Yeah," Ryan said. "We're in."

"We'll patrol the house tonight," Jimmy offered.

Lisa nodded. "Just don't let Mom or Dad catch you. And don't forget that Derek will be watching outside."

"Let's synchronize watches," Scott said. "Mine has a timer."

They divided the night into two-hour segments with Fiona and Jimmy taking the first watch at midnight.

"Wear pajamas," Lisa advised. "That way you can pretend you got up to go to the bathroom or something. And no water guns."

Ryan scowled. "I thought we were going to use these."

"Tomorrow," Fiona promised. "If this works, you'll use them tomorrow."

"Why don't you go to bed," Lisa said. "You'll need the sleep."

"No way," Ryan argued. "Come on, men. Let's scout the perimeter."

The boys took off outside, water guns dripping.

"I hope they don't blow it," Lisa said. "They still think this is a game."

Fiona looked out across the passage, thinking about the pirates that used to sail the calm water. She shut her eyes and tried to send her mom a picture of the deep purple silhouette of the mountains as the sun sank in the sky. She thought, maybe, she got through.

She sighed and opened her eyes. The evening was so peaceful, it seemed unbelievable that somewhere not far away, someone was planning to break into the house.

"I'm going to get flashlights," Lisa said.

"I'll come with you."

In the kitchen, Mrs. Glee was putting a bowl into the fridge. "No snacks," she barked when she saw them.

"Just getting a flashlight," Lisa said. "Fiona and I are going down to the beach and we don't want to get lost."

Mrs. Glee sniffed and untied her apron. "If you see Marcus down there, tell him I could use his help getting out the extra chairs."

"Sure," Fiona agreed.

The girls went outside and headed down toward the beach.

"Yow!" Fiona yelped. A cold stream of water doused her hair. A second stream hit Lisa on the leg.

"You guys die!" Lisa yelled.

"In your dreams!" Jimmy crawled out from under a thick clump of shrubs. Ryan came from the corner of the house.

Another thin stream of water sopped Fiona's shirt. Scott swung down from his perch in one of the madrona trees. Laughing, the boys converged on them.

"You idiots!" Lisa snapped.

"Can't take a little water?" Ryan pumped his fist a couple of times.

"We're working out our ambush," Jimmy explained.

"For everybody, including the thief, to see and hear!" Fiona said. "This isn't about pretending to be soldiers."

The boys looked abashed.

"But nobody's around," Scott protested.

"Hi, kids!" The five spun around as Bruce walked out of the shadows. He eyed the fluorescent water guns. "Catch anything?"

Ryan scowled. "Not yet. But we aren't finished."

"Forget your trimmer again?" Lisa asked.

Bruce's eyes narrowed. "Your mom wants the grounds cleaned up for her party. Probably take me half the night. I swear these blackberries grow a foot a day." He hefted his clippers.

"What about Marcus?" Fiona asked. "If he

helped, you'd get it done easy. You wouldn't have to hang around."

Bruce shrugged. "He says he's got plans."

The gardener strolled across the lawn toward another hump of encroaching blackberry canes.

Fiona watched him. "Bruce sure is keen all of a sudden."

Lisa lifted her chin. "It doesn't matter if it's him or somebody else – once we spring the trap."

It might matter, Fiona thought. *If they'd somehow alerted a professional thief.* Looking around at her brother and cousins, she felt a quiver of fear.

"Are you coming?" Lisa called from the door.

Shaking off her anxious thoughts, Fiona followed the others into the house.

That night she lay silently in bed, trying not to worry, listening for the sound of lights being switched off and doors being locked in Uncle Harold's nighttime routine. She glanced at the clock. 12:15.

Finally the hall light flicked off.

"Ready?" Lisa whispered from across the room.

Fiona sat up. "I'll give him fifteen minutes to go to sleep."

Lisa yawned and rolled over. "Wake me up when it's my shift."

A few minutes later, Fiona slipped into the boys' room. Jimmy was sound asleep.

"Jimmy!" She hissed and shook him.

"I'll take his turn," Ryan whispered. He slipped out of bed. As they'd agreed, he was in pajamas, but he had added a bandanna tied commando-style around his head.

Fiona sighed. "Try to remember we're under cover," she whispered.

Ryan grinned. "Trust me."

"I'm trying to," Fiona retorted softly.

Together they crept downstairs, freezing into immobility when a floorboard creaked. Fiona pointed Ryan toward the living room. She went into Uncle Harold's study and checked the windows. Locked.

They met in the hall. Ryan gave a thumbs up.

One by one, they ghosted through the rooms, checking windows and locks. After the third round, they settled into easy chairs in the living room. Fiona checked her watch. 1:17. She'd had no idea sentry duty was so boring...

Fiona jerked awake and blinked. How could she have dozed off! She glanced at her watch. 1:38. Okay...she hadn't been asleep too long. In the chair beside her, Ryan softly snored.

Fiona shivered. She should have put on socks. Her feet were icy cold from the draft....

She swallowed. "Ryan!" she whispered.

He stirred, but didn't wake up. Fiona sat still, straining to hear a sound. Any sound that didn't belong.

What was that? Fiona took long slow breaths. She had to do something.

Forcing herself to stand up, she stole across the floor. Her bare feet made no sound. Only her breathing and pounding heart echoed loudly in her ears. She followed the cold air into the family room...one of the French doors was half-open.

Fiona ran toward it, ready to slam it against any intruder. She froze. Outside on the patio, two dark figures rolled across the stones, each grunting and grappling for a hold. Derek's dog, Pixie, barked and lunged at the fighters. Then the man with sandy hair managed to pin down the other. Pixie whined and danced around them.

"Bruce!" Fiona hissed.

The gardener stared at her, swore softly, and then yanked his adversary to his feet.

"Derek!" Fiona gasped. She stared from one to the other, not sure what to do.

Derek shoved hard, trying to get loose, but the older man held him tight.

"I caught him!" Derek snarled. "He was breaking into the house."

Bruce gave him a shake. "You idiot! I caught you this time, jimmying the lock. You got away from me earlier but you had to come back and try again. And this time I got you!"

"I didn't! You're lying!" Derek snapped. "I caught *you!*"

Fiona stepped back and slammed the door on them. Breathing hard, she ran upstairs to her bedroom and shut that door too. She dove into bed and pulled up the covers. Her feet were freezing. Her heart was pounding, and she was shaking from more than the cold.

She'd caught the thief – she just didn't know who it was.

Chapter 17

The Waiting Game

"Pink, red, green, yellow or orange?" Fiona read off the labels.

"Just plain glow-in-the dark," Lisa replied. She picked a bottle of paint powder from the shelf of the artists supply store. "The powder will be white unless it gets wet. Then it will be brilliant!"

"Did we forget anything?" Fiona checked the basket again. It was filled with boxes of chalk and jars of powdered paint.

"I don't see how. We've gone over this plan about twenty times."

Their council of war had lasted nearly an hour. Ryan, Jimmy and Scott were furious that Fiona hadn't woken them up. They didn't get that she had been too shocked...and too scared. Fiona didn't know what she should have done, but in daylight, she ashamedly decided there must have been something better to do than hide in her bed.

She'd expected Lisa to be angry too, but her cousin just shook her head.

"It's got to be Bruce," Lisa told them. "But the cops would believe anything he tells them because they're sure Derek is guilty. Tonight we'll trap the real thief with proof – and then Derek will be cleared."

Fiona nodded and said nothing. But she wondered uneasily if maybe Derek had been telling the lies. She wasn't certain about anything now.

Their trap had to work!

"Are you sure we have enough chalk?"

Lisa dropped another jar of paint powder into their basket. "We've got fourteen boxes. The store doesn't have any more."

The girl at the checkout eyed them in surprise as Lisa dumped box after box of chalk on the counter.

"Um...we play a lot of hopscotch," Fiona told her.

"I guess you do." She rang up the total and watched bemused as they filled the backpack Fiona had brought.

Taking turns carrying the bag, the girls headed back toward Vickers Villa at a fast walk.

In the kitchen, Aunt Irene and Mrs. Glee were taking cut flowers from florists' boxes and arranging them carefully in several waiting vases.

The girls silently eased into the pantry.

"I think a white spray of whatever these are..." Aunt Irene was saying. Mrs. Glee handed her a flower stalk and they both stared critically at the arrangement.

"A little more greenery, Mrs. V...?"

Quietly, Lisa opened a cupboard and took out a couple of big jars.

"Are you sure about this?" Fiona whispered.

"Trust me," Lisa replied. "Keep a look-out."

"There...that's just lovely. The upstairs hall, don't you think?" Aunt Irene said happily. Arms full of the bouquets, the women left.

Fiona gave the thumbs up signal to her cousin, crossed the kitchen and stationed herself by the hall door.

Lisa dropped a handful of chalk into the food blender and hit the button. The roar was deafening. But within seconds the chalk had churned into powder.

Working fast, Lisa dumped the white dust into a jar. Then she dropped in more handfuls of chalk. With a jab of the puree button, those ground into powder too.

The sixth batch was roaring away when Aunt Irene and Mrs. Glee sailed downstairs. Fiona ran to meet them.

"What's going on in there?" Mrs. Glee demanded.

"Milkshakes," Fiona gasped quickly. "Lisa's making protein shakes! Energy and...and nutrition!"

"Mrs. Vickers, how can I get ready with the girls messing around?" complained Mrs. Glee.

"Oh my...I mean, girls, we can't disturb Mrs. Glee," Aunt Irene said. "There is so much to do..."

"That's why we came in when you were busy," Fiona said sweetly. "But we were so hungry...growing girls, you know."

"Oh dear...they do have to eat, Mrs. Glee... but, what's wrong with the blender? Why is it making that dreadful noise?" Aunt Irene peered over Fiona's shoulder.

"Um...it's a health food shake," Fiona said quickly. "You know, pine nuts and...and sunflowers seeds and...things."

Aunt Irene frowned. The blender roared again.

"That doesn't sound very nice..." Aunt Irene said. "And really, today of all days, you shouldn't be in the kitchen...."

The doorbell rang.

"I'll get it," Mrs. Glee snapped. "Seeing as my kitchen's being used."

"Oh dear..." Aunt Irene said. She followed the housekeeper toward the door.

Fiona dashed into the kitchen. "Saved by the bell."

"This is the last one." Lisa pointed to the nearly full jars. Rapidly Fiona stuffed them into the backpack.

"Got them! Let's get out of here!" Fiona urged.

Too late. Aunt Irene and Mrs. Glee came back into the kitchen.

"This is wonderful," Aunt Irene exclaimed holding up a recipe card. "Mrs. Bocci sent over her special recipe for blender custard sauce to make a trifle."

"I made cherry pies," Mrs. Glee snapped. "And she should have sent it over a week ago when you asked her."

Aunt Irene frowned. "Oh...I see...but I don't want to offend Caroline by not using her recipe. Perhaps...well...I can make it."

Mrs. Glee feigned deafness. The girls watched helplessly as Aunt Irene cracked four eggs into a bowl and dumped them into the blender.

"Lisa, did you rinse it?" Fiona whispered.

Lisa shook her head. "I didn't have time."

"I think our plan just got more complicated," Fiona sighed.

Lisa giggled. "Or Mrs. Bocci's recipe for custard won't be in demand any more."

Four hours later, Lisa opened their bedroom door a crack and peered down the hall one more time.

"Mom still isn't finished dressing," she reported.

Fiona readjusted her beaded hair clips and tried to pat down the wild mass of her freshly washed hair. Just for once, she wished her hair would slide into place the way Lisa's did.

"Aunt Irene will be ready soon," she said, turning away from the mirror. "She's got to be. The party's supposed to start now."

As if in response, the doorbell chimed.

"Oh dear..." Aunt Irene hurried out of her room.

The girls exchanged looks of triumph and opened their bedroom door wider.

"Lisa! Fiona!" Aunt Irene stopped by their door. "Thank goodness you're ready. The caterer sent the food, but the waitress I hired hasn't come. I need you to help pass around the hors d'oeuvres."

"But...um...we were going to check on the boys," Fiona said.

"They're fine. They have loads of snacks and they're playing some kind of video game in Scott's room," Aunt Irene said. "And I really need you."

"Sure, Mom," Lisa agreed. With a mutual look of resignation, the girls followed her downstairs.

In the kitchen, Mrs. Glee handed each of them a silver tray filled with tiny appetizers. "When those are gone, there's more in those pans over there." She indicated several loaded cookie sheets on top of the stove. "And in those boxes from the caterer. I've got to see to the door."

The girls nodded and carried their trays into the living room. More people had arrived and the doorbell was still chiming. Aunt Irene beamed and introduced her daughter and niece as the guests streamed in.

Uncle Harold shook hands and directed people to the alcove where a bartender was mixing drinks.

The trays quickly emptied. Fiona returned to the kitchen for a refill. Lisa was arranging parsley on her stacked tray.

"Mom's party looks like a big success," Lisa said.

"That's great," Fiona replied. "But what about our plan?"

"Fiona, dear," Aunt Irene called from the door to the living room. "Could you bring around another tray?"

"Sure thing, Aunt Irene. I'm just refilling my tray," Fiona called.

Her aunt disappeared.

"What are we going to do?" Fiona began loading her serving dish with hors d'oeuvres.

Lisa helped herself to a sausage roll. "Let's take in one more tray each, then just disappear."

"What if your Mom comes to look for us?" Fiona asked.

Lisa shrugged. "I don't know what else to do."

Just then the kitchen door opened and Marcus came in, carrying a black plastic tackle box.

"Marcus!" Fiona turned to him. "Can you help us out?"

The boy hesitated. "I just came in for my bait. Stored it in your fridge."

"With the party food?" Lisa wrinkled her nose. "Why not use your own fridge?"

"It's broken," he said impatiently. "Look, what do you want me to do?"

Fiona shoved a stack of trays toward him. "Fill these with hors d'oeuvres."

Marcus shrugged and put down the tackle box. "Sure. Why not?"

The girls grabbed the hors d'oeuvres and headed for the living room. The laughing and chattering guests weren't grabbing them as quickly now. And Mrs. Glee seemed to have left her post by the door. She came in from the kitchen, carrying a freshly filled platter.

Fiona put her serving dish on a convenient table. "Now's our chance," she whispered to Lisa.

Her cousin nodded and left her tray on another table. They smiled at everyone and slipped out of the room and up the staircase.

The hallway was dark and the sounds from the party downstairs were muffled. From under her bed, Lisa got the backpack and flashlight. The boys crowded around the door into their room.

"Ready?" Lisa asked.

"Yeah," Scott answered. "We've got it all worked out." Ryan and Jimmy nodded.

"You guys keep watch," Fiona told them.

Ryan gave a thumbs up and the boys silently took up posts by the staircase. Scott went down half way, ready to signal if someone headed upstairs. The girls slipped into the darkened master bedroom. Fiona snapped on her flashlight.

"Where's the jewelry box?" she asked.

Lisa pointed to the dressing table. "Over there."

They skirted the four poster bed and went over to Aunt Irene's dressing table. Fiona shone the flashlight over a silver-backed hairbrush set, a collection of cut glass perfume decanters arranged on a lace doily, and then across the jewelry box.

Using one finger, Fiona lifted the lid. Pearls, gold, rings, and a diamond bracelet winked up at her.

"Wow!" Fiona whispered.

"Grandma Vickers and her sister, Great Aunt Lisa, left Mom all their jewelry," Lisa explained in a low voice. "There's even more in here." She crossed the dark room and swung a painting to one side, revealing the safe hidden behind it.

A wave of laughter rose from downstairs. Fiona and Lisa jumped.

"Can you open it?" Fiona whispered.

Lisa punched in the combination, and pulled open the metal door revealing several pale velvet jewelers boxes. Fiona took out one of the jars of paint powder and unscrewed the cap. While Lisa held the jewelry cases open, Fiona dashed liberal puffs of paint powder into the back of the safe and over the gems.

"Done!"

Lisa pushed the door shut and swung the picture back into place.

"Easy on the jewelry box," Lisa whispered. "Too much might show."

She held up the lid and took out the pieces of jewelry. Fiona shook the jar until the box's white velvet lining was thick with powder. Then Lisa put back the jewelry and closed the lid.

"Oh, Aunt Irene!" Jimmy yelled out in the hallway.

Fiona and Lisa froze.

"Don't go in there!" bellowed Ryan.

"We're dead," Fiona gasped.

"Why, boys...what's the matter?" Aunt Irene did not sound pleased. "I need to freshen my makeup."

"Don't do that," Jimmy insisted. "Fiona's in there."

"I'll kill him," his sister snarled.

"Fiona's in my room?" Aunt Irene sounded even more bewildered.

"And Lisa..." Ryan added.

"I'll help you," Lisa hissed.

"I was sick." Scott's voice took on angelic tones. "Real sick. And I used your bathroom...I kind of missed the toilet."

"We're looking after him," Ryan reported. "Fiona and Lisa are cleaning up."

"Oh, dear...Scott, should you go to bed? Fiona? Lisa...is everything all right?" Aunt

Irene's face peered around the doorpost. "Do you want some lights?"

"*No!*" Lisa and Fiona yelled together.

"It's much too gross!" Fiona said. "You just wouldn't believe it."

Lisa ran to the door and blocked her mother's view. "We're okay, Mom. Just go back to the party and enjoy yourself."

"All right," Aunt Irene said dubiously. She turned to the boys. "But why didn't you use the toilet in your own room, Scott?"

"Jimmy was taking a dump," Scott said.

"Oh, dear...I see. Well, if you're sure you're all right." She touched her son's forehead. "No fever...."

"Don't worry, Aunt Irene," Ryan said.

With another anxious glance, Aunt Irene went back downstairs.

"Good thinking, guys," Fiona said. "Are you ready?"

Jimmy nodded. "You bet."

The girls took a few more minutes to shake the rest of the paint powder and chalk into the white rug. Clouds of dust swirled into the air. They coughed and choked.

"Perfect!" Fiona wheezed. "Nothing looks different."

"Now what?" Lisa asked tensely. "Should we go downstairs?"

Fiona hesitated. "Aunt Irene won't expect us to. If we stay in here, we'll be witnesses."

"That's boring," Scott said. "Guys, let's play some more games until the robber shows up." The three cousins headed back down the hall.

Choking and wheezing from the scattered powder, the girls looked for somewhere to hide, and finally slid under the big four poster bed. Lying on their backs, staring up at the springs, they could hear the laughing and noise from the party below them.

"Everybody's having a good time," Lisa whispered. "They're getting noisier."

"Shh!"

The girls waited. Fiona stretched a foot that cramped. Lisa dozed off. Fiona tried to keep awake by remembering every book she'd ever read. She was somehow stacking fluorescent orange books on the shelves of a gigantic library when a soft thud woke her up.

She jerked up, banging her head on the frame above her.

"Ouch!"

"What the..."

Lisa elbowed her. Too late.

Fiona crawled forward to the edge of the bed. A silhouette showed against the hallway door. The burglar sprinted from the room.

"Stop!" Fiona shouted, dragging herself out from under the bed.

"Dad!" Lisa shrieked.

"Uncle Harold! Call the cops," Fiona bellowed. The girls tore out of the room, and crashed into the boys.

"It worked!" Lisa pointed. White footprints gleamed on the grey hall carpet.

"Let's get him!" Ryan yelled.

The boys unslung their water guns and raced downstairs. The girls pelted after them. The footprints disappeared in the marble entry hall.

"Uncle Harold!" Fiona cried. "Someone stole the jewelry!"

The noise from the party stopped suddenly.

"What?" Uncle Harold demanded.

"It's the thief!" Scott yelled. "He broke in!"

Uncle Harold raced up the stairs. Aunt Irene followed.

"No, Dad!" Lisa shouted. "Call the police! He's getting away!"

"Too late," Fiona groaned. "It's too late!"

Chapter 18

Glow in the Dark

Aunt Irene's screams floated down. The guests milled nervously around the living room. A few men started up the stairs.

"They're messing up the footprints!" Fiona cried.

"Quick!" Lisa ordered. "Before we have chalk prints all over the house – find some that go out a door or window!"

"Right!"

The kids split up and ran to check the house.

"Got them!" Fiona shouted. White footprints gleamed on the carpet of Uncle Harold's study. The French windows were wide open.

Fiona peered out. Not even moonlight eased the shadows. Then suddenly Pixie began barking fiercely. Shouts rose from the lawn below.

"This way!" Fiona yelled. She dove out the window and tore down the lawn. Lisa and the boys raced close behind.

In the distance police sirens wailed. Ahead, Pixie whimpered.

Lights switched on, flooding the lawn with a sudden glare. Two figures rolled and struggled on the ground.

"I got him, Mr. Vickers!" Marcus shouted. He heaved up from the grass, dragging Derek with him.

Derek shook his head groggily and tried to swing at Marcus. Pixie barked and growled. Everyone from the party spilled out onto the lawn. From the corner of her eye, Fiona caught sight of Bruce. He leaned over to pick up Marcus' plastic tackle box.

Staring at it, Fiona froze.

Lisa ran to Derek and tried to drag Marcus away.

Bruce shoved the box into Fiona's hands and pulled the boys apart. Ryan, Jimmy and Scott whooped and shot sprays of water at them.

"Stop it!" Lisa shrieked.

Derek held his face where blood dripped from a cut above his eye and mingled eerily with a dab of fluorescent paint. He and Marcus both struggled in Bruce's grip.

Uncle Harold grabbed Derek's arms and held him.

"I didn't do it!" Derek cried. "I was trying to help!"

"No! It isn't Derek," Lisa sobbed. "It isn't. He's my friend."

Fiona slowly unsnapped the lid of the tackle box. Aunt Irene's jewelry, smeared with fluorescent paint powder, rattled in the bottom.

"Lisa," Uncle Harold said gently. "Marcus caught him red-handed."

There was a sudden silence as everyone looked from the box to Derek.

"Red-handed..." Fiona said slowly. "That's it!"

She pounded Ryan's shoulder and pointed at Marcus. "Get him!" she yelled.

"All right!" The boys shouted war cries and shot stream after stream of water at both boys. Derek held up his hands to stop the flood of water.

"Hey!" Marcus yelled, trying to twist away. "Cut it out!"

Neither boy could avoid the three-way spray.

Marcus wiped his hands over his streaming face and tried to dry them on his pants. Under the floodlights, fluorescent paint shone as it dripped across his chin, streaked his jeans, and pooled around his shoes.

"Marcus is the thief!" Fiona shouted. "He's glowing in the dark! We got him!"

"The paint," Lisa tugged at her father's arm. "It's proof, Dad! We booby-trapped the jewelry!"

Marcus stared down at his glowing hands and then looked up, his eyes blazing. He spun on his heel and sprinted toward the dock.

"Stop him!" Fiona shouted.

Bruce swore and raced down the steps after him.

The boathouse door slammed. The motorboat spluttered...then abruptly died.

Ignoring the excited chatter of the party guests, Fiona held up the tackle box. "This is the clue we were trying to figure out. The first time I saw Marcus going fishing – before we found the treasure – he had this box. Not the old metal one."

"When he saw we'd found the stashed treasure under the pier, he got his metal box back and filled it with fishing gear," Lisa exclaimed. "If we had taken the box with his Dad's initials in the first place, Marcus would have been nailed."

"But we got him anyway!" Fiona grinned.

Police sirens wailed loudly. Two cars pulled into the driveway. Sergeant Reese and three policemen ran down the lawn just as Bruce pulled Marcus up the steps.

"Get out of my way!" A loud voice rasped over the lawn. Mrs. Glee pushed her way forward.

"What are you doing!" she demanded of the officers.

"Your son robbed us," Mr. Vickers told her.

"Mom," Marcus cried. His thin face was pale. "Tell them it's a mistake!"

"Oh no..." Her eyes filled. "Oh, my boy...."

"Where's the rest of the jewelry?" Bruce demanded.

Marcus took a deep breath, almost a sob. "Under my bed."

"So, Lansford, you were right," Sergeant Reese said. He took Marcus' arm. "Let's go, son." He escorted him up to the police cars, helped him into the back seat, and watched as the officers drove away.

"I have to go with him," Mrs. Glee cried.

Uncle Harold put his arm around her. "I'll drive you." They went up to the house.

"So, that's the end of my career as a really terrible gardener," Bruce announced. "Thank goodness."

"You're a policeman!" Fiona accused.

He grinned. "Guilty. I was brought in from Seattle. A lot of influential people live around here and they don't like being the target of a crime wave."

"Why didn't you leave when they arrested Derek?" Lisa asked.

Bruce shrugged. "Reese wanted me to, but I didn't think Derek was guilty."

Derek grinned. "Thanks."

"No problem." Bruce smiled at the girls. "I was just about sure this house would be the next target, but until you two started investigating, I hadn't found a single clue to the real thief."

"What about the reward?" Fiona held her breath.

"You kids will get all the credit," Bruce promised.

"Yes!" Fiona raised her fist in triumph.

"Lansford!" Sergeant Reese strode back from the driveway. "We have to get down to the station. You've got a lot of paperwork waiting for you."

"See you around, kids." Bruce took the tackle box and left with the Sergeant.

"C'mon guys," Ryan said. "Let's see if the cops are going to interrogate anybody."

The boys ran up the lawn. Talking excitedly, the guests began to wander back too.

Fiona watched. "I almost wish we hadn't caught Marcus. Poor Mrs. Glee."

"Seems hard to believe it was him all along." Derek agreed. "But at least now everyone knows

I'm innocent. It's his first offence. Maybe it'll straighten him out."

"I hope so," Lisa said. Derek hugged her.

Fiona rolled her eyes. "I'm going back in. Aunt Irene's trifle isn't such a big hit. It's time to break out the cherry pies."

Lisa didn't seem to even hear her.

When Fiona finally got up the next morning, breakfast had been laid on the patio and Uncle Harold was tapping notes on his tablet, as usual. What was not usual was the company. Derek sat at the table between Lisa and Aunt Irene.

"Coming through!" Ryan pushed past Fiona with a plate of bacon.

"Watch out!" Scott swung by with a plastic bowl of strawberries.

"Get out of the way, Fiona!" Jimmy cried. He carried a tray loaded with mugs and a coffee pot.

"No fuss, no muss." Ryan declared, surveying the scene.

The boys helped themselves to breakfast, then raced down on the lawn to eat.

Aunt Irene groped for the coffee.

"Morning!" Fiona said.

"Oh, good morning, dear," Aunt Irene said. She turned to Derek. "I'm so glad you joined us...." She blushed. "I'm afraid...I didn't treat you very well and I'm sorry."

"It's okay," Derek said, blushing himself. "Between Ginger spreading rumors and Marcus framing me with my own jacket, I looked pretty bad. Lisa was the only one who believed in me."

"And Fiona," she said.

Fiona grinned. "Most of the time."

"I can't believe it was Marcus," Lisa said.

Uncle Harold poured himself some coffee. "It was clear from what he said to the police, that Marcus is having some real problems. He's so angry about the hard times he and his mom went through that he began to feel he deserved that jewelry he took. It's a shame, but I'm going to recommend counseling to the judge."

"Dad?" Lisa said. "You're going to represent him?"

Uncle Harold nodded and went back to tapping on his tablet.

Lisa smiled and sat back. Fiona grinned and reached for orange juice.

A few minutes later, the door to the Glee's cottage opened, and Mrs. Glee came out. Her eyes looked puffy, but she walked determinedly toward the family.

"Mrs. Vickers," she said. "I'll get my stuff packed and be out of here as quick as I can."

Fiona and Lisa exchanged looks.

"Oh dear..." Aunt Irene said. "Mrs. Glee...I don't know...." She paused. "Mrs. Glee," she said firmly. "I can't stop you from leaving, but I don't want you to go."

Uncle Harold looked up. "Irene...."

"No," Aunt Irene interrupted. "I run the household, and, Mrs. Glee," she turned to the woman, "I don't think I could manage without you."

"But what about my boy?" In spite of herself, Mrs. Glee's chin quivered slightly.

"He made a terrible mistake," Aunt Irene said. "But I've always liked Marcus and the jewelry was recovered...except for Christine Bocci's emerald bracelet.... Are you all right, dear?"

"I'm fine..." Fiona choked. "I swallowed wrong."

Uh-oh, Lisa mouthed to Fiona. Fiona giggled and started to cough again.

Aunt Irene turned back to Mrs. Glee. "I hope you'll stay."

Mrs. Glee blinked rapidly and nodded. "All right then. And thank you." She headed back to the cottage.

"I don't suppose I'll ever get a decent meal again," Uncle Harold grumbled.

Aunt Irene just smiled.

Fiona sat back and looked across the passage at the misty mountains. She thought the scene to her mom, and then sent after it waves of reassurance.

The reward money would look after her family's unpaid bills, Mom was getting better, and Fiona was planning on a long, fun summer on the Island.

...Once she and Lisa figured out how to return Mrs. Bocci's emerald bracelet!

And now a Sneak Peek at

Sammy and the Devil Dog

Everything has gone wrong in Sammy's life. Her mom is broke, she's in constant trouble at school, and the school bully is causing her trouble. When Sammy rescues an abused dog named Jack, her problems get even worse. Jack never learned to be a good dog – he's wild and unpredictable. But then the bully turns on them all.

Something's Fishy at Ash Lake
by Anne Stephenson and Susan Brown

Part time detectives and full time mischief-makers Liz Elliot & Amber Mitchell get themselves in way over their heads when an evil prankster threatens their summer vacation! They should be roasting marshmallows, not risking their lives!

"Amber!" Liz clutched Amber's arm. "Did you hear something?"

The two girls stood perfectly still, ears straining, hearts thumping through the darkness...

A shadow slipped across the floor. Soft footsteps sounded from the far side of the kitchen. The girls cowered against the wall. They could see feet, then legs. Moonlight silhouetted a dark figure by the door...

If they're not careful, Amber & Elliot's two-week stay at Ash Lake computer camp could be their last...*ever!*

Sammy and the Devil Dog

by

Susan Brown

Chapter 1

Let's See You Dance!

Sammy sat motionless, or as near to motionless as it was possible for her. Her eyes hardly left the house phone sitting on the kitchen counter. Eleven minutes before her mom came home. If the call didn't come before then, Sammy was dead...or maybe worse than dead.

Impatiently Sammy shoved her bangs out of her eyes. The movement made the bruise on her shoulder ache a little more, but she didn't care. She glanced at the clock. Nine minutes. Maybe the traffic would be bad. Maybe her mom would be delayed. Mrs. Martinez didn't have her mom's cell phone number, so the call would come here. Maybe this time Sammy would be lucky.

Lucky...not likely....

Six minutes.

Then, shattering the silence, the phone rang. Holding her breath, Sammy waited, counting the rings...*one...two...three...four...*. The answering machine picked up. *"Hi there. Sammy and Linda are dying to talk to you, but we aren't here! Leave a message. Leave a number. We'll call back!"*

"Hello, this is Tony from the Take a Stand Foundation. We're calling today..."

Sammy grabbed the receiver, held it at arms length for about three seconds and then slammed it down again. Silence. She looked at the clock.

Four minutes. Sammy drummed her fingers on the side of the table, and then lifted her head like a dog catching a distant sound.

"Oh no," she whispered. The painful rumble of her mom's old car turned into the long gravel drive.

"Oh, dirty dog, call now," she whispered, "Mrs. Martinez, call now...call now...!"

The phone rang. *One...two...three...four...*.

"Hi there. Sammy and Linda are dying to talk to you, but we aren't here! Leave a message. Leave a number. We'll call back!"

The rumbling engine suddenly stopped. The car door squealed open....

"Hello Ms. Connor. This is Jeanne Martinez, principal at Samantha's school. I'm afraid that Samantha was involved in another incident today. I'd like to schedule a meeting with you

and your daughter to see what we can do to help Samantha improve her behavior. I know there have been a lot of changes in your lives recently, but we can't allow her to continue to make such inappropriate choices. Please call me to schedule a time."

The message machine beeped. Sammy jabbed the erase button as Linda Connor pushed open the kitchen door.

"Hi Sammy, how was school?" her mom asked. "Can you help me with these bags? I can't believe how much I saved at the consignment store. I found the cutest top! I told you I had a date Saturday with a guy I met at the pottery sale, didn't I?"

When Sammy took the largest bag, her mom pulled a bright pink blouse from the other stuffed plastic bag and held it up to her chin. "What do you think?"

"It's great, mom," Sammy said. "Really a good color on you."

Her mom grinned. "Thanks, kiddo. I'm going to get cleaned up and get some work done in my studio. What are you up to?"

"Erin got back from Japan on Tuesday, so we're going to hang out," Sammy said. "Is that okay?"

Her mom was already pulling off her outer clothes before heading to the shower, but she stopped and gave Sammy a squeeze. "I'm really glad she's back. This has been a tough time for you to be by yourself, without your best friend."

Sammy hugged back. "You too."

Her mom laughed a little shakily, and ran her fingers through her hair. "That's life," she said. "It just keeps on happening whether you're ready or not. I need to get cleaned up."

Sammy smiled like the good kid she used to be, until her mom was out of sight. Then she took the house phone off its cradle, turned it on, and dropped it to the floor. In a smooth motion, she nudged it behind and under the counter.

"And stay there," Sammy said.

Problem dealt with, Sammy ran out back to get her bike. She and Erin were meeting at the convenience store. When Sammy had puffed her way up the long hill, Erin was waiting for her outside the store with two big freezies in her hands. When she tried to wave with the cups in her hand, it looked so funny, Sammy started to laugh.

Jumping off, Sammy propped her bike against the wall and took a long frozen slurp, so cold it almost burned. "Oh," she sighed blissfully, "you will be my best friend forever."

Erin giggled, took a long swallow herself, and then looked at her friend seriously.

"Did your mom understand that you couldn't help that fight?" she demanded. "That the girls were making that little kid cry by teasing him?"

"Sure," Sammy said jerking the straw up and down. "My mom's great that way."

Erin frowned. "She didn't used to be," she said slowly. "You used to always go to your grandpa."

"Well," Sammy's voice had a weird scratch to it, "he's not here so I guess she just picked it up instead."

"Oh Sammy," Erin cried. "I am such a bad friend. I am so sorry. I shouldn't have said anything. Don't be sad!"

Her eyes held such pleading that Sammy forced herself to laugh. "It's okay," she said. "Come on – let's ride somewhere."

"Your house," Erin said. "I haven't seen it."

"Yes, you have," Sammy said.

"But not when you lived there," Erin said earnestly. "I'll bet it's entirely different now. And special because you're there."

"You're going to be disappointed," Sammy said, getting back on her bike. She didn't want to go home, but then she thought of the phone under the cupboard. Her mom would be out of the shower by now, and might notice it wasn't there. And Sammy really wanted to stay out of trouble for awhile. Last week her mom had been so mad when Sammy got blamed for wrecking the class field trip – she just hadn't realized everyone had already gotten on the bus.

Glumly, Sammy leaned back on the bike, pushed off and slowly coasted away from the store letting gravity do all the work while she sipped her drink and lightly steered with one hand.

Aaw-oooo-oooo.

Sammy must have imagined the noise – it didn't belong in the trim suburb by the convenience store.

Aaw-oooo-oooo. A dog howl, mournful and low. Alone. Lonely.

Sammy jerked her head around, nearly lost her balance and just in time, swerved out of the way of a car. Her freezie spun across the road in a fizzing whirl.

Honk! The woman glared as she sped past.

"You don't own the road!" Sammy shouted. She smacked her hands on the handlebars. Erin, completely unaware, coasted down the hill.

Aaw-oooo-oooo.

Weird. This was weird. Sammy pushed back her helmet, trying to hear better. Animal cries, whimpering. And then....

Bang! Bang! Bang! Bangbangbang!

A dog yelped and cried. Laughter exploded through the air.

Sammy dropped her bike on the grass curb. The noises came from the yard that backed onto the sidewalk. A chain link fence, thick with vines, blocked her view.

The dog's cry rose again then trailed away.

Without hesitating, Sammy toe-climbed to the top of the fence. In a weedy back yard, two teenage boys were laughing so hard they could hardly stand up. A black and white dog, long-legged and shaggy, was nearly strangling himself trying to escape the chain that held him to a tree. A litter of red paper fluttered across the beaten dirt. The smell of gunpowder snagged Sammy's nostrils.

"Hey, dummy!" the tallest boy yelled to the dog. "Let's see you dance."

He held up a string of red firecrackers, struck a match, and lit the fuse. The boy threw them at the dog. The animal whimpered, leaped frantically into the air, then fell heavily as the chain nearly choked him. The crackers hissed and sputtered near his face.

"Stop!" Sammy screamed.

She leapt down from the fence and raced across the yard. The fuse was almost gone when Sammy kicked.

The first cracker went off as her toe hit the pack. She felt the smack and heard the pop. But the rest of the string flew in smooth arc back toward the boys.

"Hey!" they howled as the firecrackers popped and banged at their feet.

"How do you like dancing!" Sammy tore over to them. Firecrackers, big ones, were going off in her brain. "How could you do that? You are wicked and cruel and you deserve to die!"

"Ah shut up, you little witch!" the shorter boy snarled.

The biggest one leaned against the wall and grinned. "We weren't hurting it. But that was a good move, kid. Real good kick."

"Get off our property!" The first one glared.

"Not a chance!" Sammy jabbed her fists into her hips. "I'm going to call the police and they're going to arrest you for cruelty to animals. You were torturing that dog!"

"What torture," the tallest teenager demanded. "We're training our dog to be a watchdog. And a watchdog is no good unless it's mean."

"You're just hurting it. You can't do that!"

"Yes we can – it's our dog."

Sammy narrowed her eyes and tried to decide if she had any chance of survival if she smacked that superior grin right off his face.

What would Papa Jack have done?

"Sammy?" Erin was hanging onto the fence, peering over the top. "What's going on? Are you okay?"

"Yes, but those jerks were throwing fire crackers at him." Sammy turned to the animal. The dog was trying to hide behind the tree, pulling on his chain, making soft yelping noises. "Oh, you poor thing..."

She walked slowly toward it, holding out her hand. "He's just a puppy!" At the sound of her voice, the dog swiveled so that it crouched, nose pointing toward her.

"Oh you beautiful thing," Sammy crooned. The sun shone on the dog's rich black coat and gleamed on the long white diamond on his forehead. His two front paws and the thick ruff on his chest were clean white too. Sammy crouched and held out her hand. The dog sprang at her.

Sammy leaped back, tripped and fell. The dog stood over her, snarling. Black eyes ringed with white; black lips curled above white fangs. Sammy couldn't move, didn't dare move.

And then another boy ran past, grabbed the dog's chain and hauled him off. The dog barked and snapped.

"Shut up!" The boy smacked the dog on the head. The dog whimpered again and dropped down, head on its too-big puppy paws. The wild black eyes warmed to brown. The edge of a soft pink tongue peeked between its lips.

Sammy sat up. "Brian? Brian Haydon? What are you doing here?"

"I live here, stupid."

Sammy scrambled to her feet. "Here? I thought you lived in the apartments."

Brian shrugged. "We moved. That's why I got a dog. But he isn't any good."

Sammy took a deep breath, making the world look normal again. The pup's white-tipped tail thumped once.

"Do you know what they were doing to him?" Sammy demanded.

Brian looked up at the teenagers leaning against the wall. His face got hard. "Joe, I'm training the dog. You probably ruined him."

"Aah, what a shame," the big one, Joe, said. "You're such a woos, Brian. Besides we didn't hurt him – much. Com'on Kyle. Play you, *Die Again Sucka*, on the computer."

They banged into the house. Brian swore under his breath.

"Who are *they*?" Erin hopped down from the fence, careful to keep a long way from the dog. She pushed her helmet more securely onto her dark hair.

"My brothers." Brian's voice had a snarl in it, kind of like the dog.

"It's against the law to abuse a dog," Erin told him. "You can't do that."

"I don't abuse him," Brian muttered.

"You just hit him on the head," Sammy retorted.

Brian scowled. "You have to be strict with a dog or he won't know who his master is."

"No! Not that strict," Sammy insisted.

She walked as close as she dared to the dog. He lifted his head and growled deep in his throat. "It's okay," she said softly. "Can't you tell I'm your friend?" The dog stared at her. His tail thumped again. He cocked his head.

"What kind of dog is he?" Sammy asked.

"Mutt," Brian said. "Got him from a guy down the street when he was a puppy."

The kids studied the dog who stared back at them. "I think he's part lab," Erin said. "He's black like a lab."

"He's too big," Brian scoffed.

"And his fur is too long," Sammy agreed. "And he has white on his chest."

The dog's head lifted a little more, and this time his tail really thumped.

She crouched down, flipped her hair from her eyes, and leaned toward the dog. "You want to be friendly, don't you boy?" She held out her hand, back first, fingers curled down.

The dog stood up. His tail straightened behind him.

"Good boy," she whispered.

Quicker than she could see, he leaped. She felt his hot breath, heard the snarl in his throat and glimpsed his sharp white teeth as they closed on her bare arm.

"No!" Sammy cried. "Bad dog!"

In the background she was aware of Erin shrieking. Furious, Sammy leaned closer to the dog's face. His teeth pressed painfully on her arm and his growl was low and steady.

"You let go," she said. "You be a good dog and let go."

She felt as though her eyes had a thin line of energy connecting directly to the dog's deep brown ones. The growl rumbled slowly. The jaws tightened a little, teeth not yet breaking the skin, but soon...

"I'm not the bad guy," she whispered through gritted teeth. "I'm nice. You don't have to bite me and we can be friends. You need a friend."

The dog blinked, then suddenly yelped. Brian hauled him back roughly by the collar, and smacked him on the head again. The dog growled and bared his teeth.

"You stupid, no good dog," the boy berated him. "Drop it!" *Whack*. He smacked the dog again.

The dog backed up, lips curled and teeth gleaming in a deep snarl.

"Stop it!" Sammy yelled. "Don't you hit that dog again!"

Brian shook his head. "You got to be tough with a dog. Look how big and strong he is already. And he's only five months old. My Dad says he's a real devil. If I don't make him scared of me, what's going to make him do what I say?"

"Dogs do what you tell them because they love you!" Erin protested tearfully. "My golden retriever, Casey, does everything I tell her and she doesn't growl at me either. She loves me. She'd die for me."

Brian shrugged. "Jack was a real cute puppy. He slept with me until Dad said he had to be chained up out here and get turned into a watch dog."

Sammy thrust her chin forward. "If you hurt this dog again we'll report it to the police and you'll all get fined and go to jail."

Brian got a hard look on his face. "Ooh, I'm scared."

"I've warned you." Sammy headed to the fence, rubbing her arm. Bluish-purple tooth marks indented her skin and a line of pain crept past her elbow. The dog stared at her unblinking. "So long, boy," she said.

It took about two seconds to scramble over the fence. She rubbed her arm again. There was going to be a bruise but the dog hadn't broken the skin. He could have, couldn't he, if he wanted to? Maybe the dog didn't really want to hurt her.

"Do you think we should call the police?" Erin interrupted her thoughts.

"Maybe." Sammy picked up her bike from the grass. "Brian will beat us up at school."

"Oh, he wouldn't, because we're girls," Erin insisted.

"That's never stopped him before," Sammy said.

Brian was about six inches taller, twice as heavy and three times as strong as any other kid at Carr Elementary. When anyone, any age or size bugged him, he punched them out. Once, he'd shoved the PE teacher and pulled a five days suspension.

"Brian is disgusting – disgusting and weird." Erin tightened her helmet strap and pushed off, gliding smoothly down the bike lane.

Sammy looked back at the fence, wondering what the dog was doing now. What had Brian called him? She froze. *Jack!* The dog's name was Jack. Sammy bit her lip and pedaled slowly after her friend.

"How could Brian name his dog Jack?" she demanded.

Something's Fishy at Ash Lake

at

Susan Brown
Anne Stephenson

An Amber and Elliot Mystery

Chapter One

That Sinking Feeling

Eugene Sharkman, *a.k.a.* Jaws, hitched up his plaid shorts and surveyed the two dozen campers scattered around the computer lab. He recognized several of them from his classes at Ash Grove Junior High, including two of his grade seven students, Amber Mitchell and Liz Elliot.

"I'm pleased to see you're enjoying your first afternoon at Ash Lake's computer camp," he called above the din. "But remember, the next two weeks aren't going to be all fun and games. Programming starts tomorrow!"

A collective groan rose from the room.

"That's it. I'm out of here." Amber shut down the computerized quest they'd all been on and got up to leave.

"Hang on a minute," Liz called, eyes firmly fixed on the screen in front of her. "I'm twelve hundred points ahead!"

Amber ran her fingers through her copper-red curls and grinned. "Too late, Elliot. Looks like you've just lost your last player."

"Rats!" Liz cried in dismay, as a miniature warrior tumbled from sight. Logging off, she raced to catch up with her best friend and together they headed outside to explore their new surroundings.

The camp had been built years ago in the middle of a thick forest of pine, surrounded by stands of white ash that gave the lake its name. As the girls followed the well-worn dirt paths that criss-crossed through the trees connecting the various buildings and the beach, they could see the vibrant blue of Ash Lake shimmering ahead.

"I definitely like it here," declared Liz, as they stepped from the shade into the full glare of the sun.

"Me, too." Amber pulled a tube of sunscreen from her pocket and slathered some of it on her nose. "I just wish my freckles would stop dividing and multiplying."

"What do you think happened to Craig and Jonathan?" Liz tightened the elastic holding her dark hair in a ponytail as they plowed their way through the soft sand.

"Don't worry, they'll show. No one turns down an opportunity like this."

Eastern Technology, one of the biggest high-tech firms in the country, owned the computer camp. And Craig's father, Robert

Nicholson, was one of the company vice-presidents.

"Craig's probably giving Jonathan the royal tour." Amber bent down and tested the cool water with her fingers. Tiny pebbles glistened invitingly beneath the surface. "Let's go for a swim," she suggested.

"Didn't you see the sign?"

"What sign?"

"The one that says no unsupervised swimming." Liz pointed to a white board with red lettering affixed to the base of the lifeguard's chair.

"Does it say anything about boating?" Amber asked, her eyes on a small flotilla of colorful paddleboats bobbing gently at the dock nearby.

"Nope."

"Then let's go."

Liz hesitated a moment. "Shouldn't we have life jackets?"

"It's only a paddleboat. What could possibly go wrong?"

Shrugging, Liz followed her friend onto the wooden dock. There were about a dozen paddleboats in all. Amber chose a yellow one and hopped aboard.

"How do you work these things, anyway?" Liz asked as she cautiously climbed onto the seat beside her friend.

"Easy, it's like riding a bike. You just pedal and use this stick to steer." Amber grabbed the rudder in her left hand. "Okay, go."

The two girls pedaled furiously. The boat lurched forward and then stopped abruptly.

"Stupid thing must be broken," muttered Amber, face flushed with exertion.

"Perhaps if we untied it..."

"Aagh!"

Amber climbed back onto the dock, released the boat from its mooring, and took a flying leap onto the seat beside Liz. "Okay. Now we're ready." They started pedaling again.

"Just like riding a bike, is it?" Liz demanded several minutes later. "Four feet and three crashed boats. I think we need training wheels."

"Don't worry," Amber reassured her, "I've got the hang of it now." She swung the rudder to the right, narrowly missing another boat.

Liz giggled and pedaled harder. They zigzagged past the roped-off swimming area and headed for open water.

It was definitely cooler out on the lake. They stopped pedaling and put their feet up on the fiberglass prow. Amber closed her eyes and let the boat drift idly.

"This is the life," sighed Liz.

"You said it," Amber agreed. "No parents, no brothers, and no one to bother us."

"And no cell phones," Liz added.

"Don't remind me. How am I going to stay connected?" Amber grumbled. "They advertise a technology camp, but don't allow phones."

"I'm definitely not going to miss them," Liz said. "My mother's on hers all the time.... What's that noise? Sounds like someone crying in the distance."

"Probably a loon or something."

Liz shielded her eyes from the late afternoon sun and peered across the sparkling lake. She could see a canoe about half a mile away, with two very familiar paddlers wearing bright orange and yellow life jackets.

"Hey, look! We've got company. It's Craig and Jonathan, and they're acting very strange."

Amber opened her eyes and sat up. The two boys had raised their paddles and were gesturing wildly.

"I didn't think they'd be *that* glad to see us here," she commented. "They're even turning around."

Sure enough, the canoe had swung about and was heading towards them. Jonathan Weiss, straight up as usual, sat in the prow of the boat, with Craig Nicholson providing the muscle behind him.

"There's a white thing in the water up ahead. Do you think that could be what they're yelling about?" Liz pointed to a white plastic cone bobbing in the water a short distance away.

"It's just a marker," answered Amber. "Probably some underwater rocks there. We'll steer around it." She moved the rudder to the right and they began pedaling in a wide arc around the buoy.

"Amber, look out!"

Jagged rocks suddenly loomed beneath the surface just ahead of them. Amber viciously cranked the rudder.

"The brakes! Put on the brakes!"

"What brakes? Boats don't have brakes."

Crunch!

The fiberglass hull dragged slowly across the ragged submerged rocks. The boat lurched, came to a momentary stop, then gently drifted free.

Liz cleared her throat. "I think we have a problem."

"No kidding." Amber watched as the water slowly rose up the soles of her sneakers. "I have a sinking feeling we're about to go down with the ship."

"That's not funny," snapped Liz. "We've only been at this camp two hours and twenty-five minutes, and already we're in trouble."

"Some people might say that's an improvement," Amber retorted hotly.

They looked down at the water seeping in, looked up at each other, and then burst out laughing.

"Do you remember the time Lindsay Watson said she'd give you a quarter if you spit on Jane Dobbs's shoes?" Liz chuckled.

"Yeah," said Amber wistfully. "It was the high point of my primary school career." She laughed. "I've never seen Dobbsie so mad. She's such a snot-nose."

"I'm just glad she's not here to see this," said Liz. "She'd be on our case about it the whole vacation."

"Don't you think there's something fishy about this?" Amber swung her arm in the direction of the plastic cone. "The marker is over there, but the rocks are over here."

Liz shrugged. "Maybe it drifted loose."

"Ahoy there!" shouted Craig. "Having a little trouble?"

The sun had bleached Craig's hair a pale blonde, while Jonathan's dark curls had grown noticeably longer since the end of school.

Something's Fishy at Ash Lake   229

"The dynamic duo strikes again," called Jonathan as they drew closer.

"Yeah, a rock!" snickered Craig.

"You should have warned us!" Amber told them.

"What did you think we were waving and yelling for?" asked Jonathan, drawing his paddle from the water.

Amber stared down at her wet sneakers. Liz focused on the far shoreline.

"You know what I think, Jonathan," Craig said mischievously. "*I* think that *they* think that we like them."

"Listen, you idiot! While you're having your little joke, we're taking on water!"

"If we don't get to shore in a hurry," added Liz, "we're going to sink."

"You *can* swim, can't you?"

"Of course we can swim," said Amber through clenched braces. "Come on, Elliot, let's head for the dock."

"You guys don't have a bailing can, do you?" Liz asked calmly.

"*Elliot!*"

"Just thought I'd ask."

Amber turned the rudder and the girls began to pedal again, steering a wide, erratic course around the rocks. The water in the boat had risen past their ankles, making it harder and harder to pedal.

"This'll be the shortest camp holiday on record," huffed Liz. "I don't think my allowance will cover a boat."

"Then pedal harder! If this thing sinks, we might as well pack up and head for home."

The boys slipped alongside in their canoe.

"Camp just wouldn't be the same without you," observed Craig. "Better, maybe."

Both boys laughed. The girls stopped pedaling and glared at them.

"Still, the boat's worth saving," added Jonathan. "We'd better tow them to shore."

The boys maneuvered in front of the laboring boat. Craig grabbed the mooring line and tied it to the stern of the canoe.

"You two keep pedaling and we'll paddle," he instructed.

At first they barely moved. Then as they gained momentum, the paddleboat wallowed after the green canoe.

"This is humiliating," muttered Liz.

They had almost made it to shore when a young woman dressed in the camp T-shirt, khaki shorts, and a baseball cap walked onto the beach. She paused for a moment, staring out at the two boats and their occupants, then strode out onto the dock.

"Oh, no," groaned Liz. "Who's that?"

"Kelly Slemko, the athletic director," said Craig over his shoulder.

"Is that good or bad?" asked Amber.

Jonathan shrugged. "She seemed okay to me."

"What's going on here?" demanded the director as the paddleboat bumped gently into the dock.

"We, uh, hit a rock," Liz confessed. "Craig and Jonathan helped us in."

"Are you all right?"

The girls nodded. "Shouldn't those rocks be marked though?" asked Amber. "We could have really run into trouble."

Kelly stared down at her in surprise. "All the dangerous rocks in the lake are marked."

"Those ones weren't."

"That's ridiculous. I checked them only yesterday." The athletic director looked at Craig and Jonathan for verification.

"Amber's right," Jonathan told her as he and Craig put up their paddles and clambered onto the dock. "The buoys are all out of position."

"We tried to warn them," said Craig.

Kelly Slemko turned back to Amber and Liz. "Jonathan and Craig asked my permission to take out the canoe," she said pointedly, "but I don't remember giving it to you two."

"We, uh, didn't know we needed permission," offered Liz.

"Haven't you read the camp handbook yet?"

"We just got here," Amber protested.

"We were going to get to it tonight..." Liz faltered.

"What are your names, and what cabins are you in?"

"Amber Mitchell, Cabin Three."

"Liz Elliot, Cabin Three, too."

"Well, Amber and Liz, when you have read the handbook you'll know that no boats are to be taken out without permission." Kelly paused and looked each of them in the eyes in turn. "And *not* without life jackets."

"Oh."

Amber opened her mouth to protest, but thought better of it. The athletic director was right. Going without life jackets had been dumb.

The paddleboat was now almost completely immersed. Kelly pursed her lips. "Just get this boat out of the lake before it sinks, girls. And for your sakes, I hope the crack in the hull can be fixed." She gave them a brisk nod and left the dock, heading up the path through the trees.

"I'd feel better if she had yelled at us," said Liz.

"Me, too." Amber stood up, water sloshing around her legs. "These boats probably cost a lot of money."

The two girls slipped over the side and into the waist-high water. With the boys pulling on the paddleboat's mooring line, they managed to push it out of the water and up onto the beach.

Jonathan prodded the hull of the damaged boat with his foot. "It's not that bad. Fiberglass can be patched and repainted. Shouldn't cost too much."

"I hope not," Craig said. "My dad told me if the camp doesn't at least break even this year, the company will sell it." He bent down and fingered the jagged edge of the crack.

"But that's crazy," interjected Amber. "The camp's part of Eastern Technology's educational program. And we get a course credit for it."

"They still have to make money," Jonathan pointed out.

Liz pulled off her wet sneakers and tossed them onto the beach. "They wouldn't send us home for this, would they?"

Jonathan put his arm around her reassuringly. "I'm sure that as long as the vice-president of finance doesn't know about you two, it'll be okay. Won't it, Craig?"

"Maybe if I put in a good word for them," drawled Craig. He straightened up just as Amber's water-logged sneaker flew across the prow of the paddleboat.

"I think it's time to go, Craig," advised Jonathan.

"Yeah, it must be almost dinnertime." Craig gave the girls a last salute, then the two boys trotted across the beach in the direction of the cabins, leaving the girls fuming in their wake.

"Those guys really irritate me," Amber grunted as she and Liz heaved the boat over. The water sloshed out and made brown sugar patterns before disappearing into the sand.

Liz leaned against the hull of the overturned boat and stared after the boys. "I think someone should take the wind out of their sails, don't you, Amber?"

"The sooner the better."

Liz gave her a brisk nod. "Agreed. Tonight after campfire."

Amber retrieved her sneaker, and the two girls picked their way carefully back to the camp in their bare feet.

ABOUT THE AUTHOR

Adventure, mystery, and magic propel Susan Brown, fuelling her imagination into writing more and more stories for her favorite audience of kids and teens.

Susan lives with her two border collie rescue dogs amid wild woods and overgrown gardens in Snohomish, Washington. From there she supervises her three daughters, assorted sons-in-law and two grandsons. It's a great way to be a writer!

Find more information, free stories, and news about upcoming books at: www.susanbrownwrites.com

Susan is also one half of Stephanie Browning, the pen name shared with her writing partner of close to a thousand years, Anne Stephenson. www.stephaniebrowningromance.com

Made in the USA
Columbia, SC
30 October 2018